30

SALT CREEK KILLING

Boredom had recently driven Rudy
Girton, town marshal of Salt Creek
City, to the bottle when a well-to-do
hotel visitor died by a murderer's
knife. A train robbery two years
earlier figured in Rudy's investigation
along with the missing family of the
knife victim. As soon as Rudy met
the missing daughter, he knew he
had to take on a whole gang of
outlaws . . . whatever the outcome.

DAVID HORSLEY

SALT CREEK KILLING

Complete and Unabridged

LINFORD
Leicester

First published in Great Britain

First Linford Edition
published 1996

British Library CIP Data

Horsley, David, *1920 –*
Salt Creek killing.—Large print ed.—
Linford western library
1. English fiction—20th century
I. Title
823.9′14 [F]

ISBN 0–7089–7911–4

Published by
F. A. Thorpe (Publishing) Ltd.
Anstey, Leicestershire

Set by Words & Graphics Ltd.
Anstey, Leicestershire
Printed and bound in Great Britain by
T. J. Press (Padstow) Ltd., Padstow, Cornwall

This book is printed on acid-free paper

1

IT was midnight. Occasionally an owl hooted, or a flea-ridden dog trotted along the rutted street of Salt Creek City, yapping fitfully. The customers in the saloons had long since stopped drinking and mulling over their recent exploits and gone to their beds.

Here and there lamps still blossomed outside buildings. The moon showed an anaemic glow in a starless sky. Early summer had drained the stamina out of the residents of the western town, so that they retired without seeking an excuse for carousing.

The bulky male silhouette which flitted along the sidewalk moved with noiseless ease, pausing a few feet short of the inviting entrance to the clapboard building known as the Salt Creek Hotel. For the size of the town, it was an imposing three-storey edifice which boasted narrow balconies outside the upper rooms fronting onto the street.

A bearded elderly male snored behind the reception counter, giving an eerie atmosphere to the foyer. The prowler waited for a whole minute before catfooting through the foyer and mounting the stairs. Moccasins muffled his feet, and a dark hat with a wide turned-down brim hid the features.

Although he was only interested in one room, the prowler studied all the other rooms which gave into the corridor of the first floor. Having ascertained to his satisfaction that no one was active behind the other doors, he moved to the one marked No. 1, and there used his acute hearing to make sure it was not occupied.

The door was locked, but he had not risked unhooking the key from the board located behind the foyer sleeper. Consequently, he removed from his pocket a special gadget, inserted a strip of metal into the door-lock, and effected an entry without any undue delay. When he was through the door, he closed it again, standing just inside and savouring the atmosphere. There was a faint smell of mothballs, offset by the faintly-perfumed odour of some expensive hair fixative.

A fancy tooled-leather money-belt hung over the head of the single bed on the near side of a hanging, drawn curtain which had the effect of partitioning the roomy bedroom.

The intruder moved to the foot of the bed and peered round it, noting two or three tailored suits hanging in a recess and an expensive valise standing on its end near them. He began to breathe more deeply, and yet he remained silent.

On the far side of the bed he crouched and looked underneath it. The screening drapes on the walk-in windows moved fractionally as a brief, ephemeral light breeze penetrated the room from the balcony.

Hauling out the smaller valise from under the bed the intruder emitted a grunt of satisfaction. It was not locked, and some of its contents greatly interested him. He tossed out two or three items onto the bed-cover. As he did so, a dog howled in the street. Unknown to the prowler, a figure stirred in a light relaxing chair on the balcony.

Presently, the sleeper on the balcony came near to full wakefulness. He heard the slight, vague noises in his room, and that sharpened his senses still more. He wrapped his robe more closely around himself, rose from the chair and stepped in through the access window.

The items tossed on the bed first caught his attention. Before he set eyes on the intruder, he gave out a sharp exclamation and fumbled around in the pocket of his robe for a small Derringer pistol.

"What in tarnation is goin' on here?"

As soon as he was aware of the man from the balcony, the intruder had backed off and flattened himself against the flimsy dividing curtain. It shielded him for a second or two: long enough for him to react to being observed.

The pocket pistol had scarcely cleared the garment when the intruder lunged forward and buried the narrow blade of a knife between the ribs on the left side of his victim's chest. A sharp intake and exhalation of breath marked the knife attack. The dying man's collapse was eased by a powerful arm as he sank to the floor.

The encounter was short-lived. After standing quite still and breathing hard for upwards of a minute, the killer stepped out onto the balcony and seated himself in the vacated chair for long enough to be sure that no one on the street was aware of the recent happening.

He then stepped back indoors and began a more thorough examination of the dead man's belongings. He had recovered from the shock of being disturbed, and this time nothing occurred to distract him.

The high-pitched shriek of the bulky female Mexican room-cleaner shattered the peace of the hotel around eight o'clock the following morning. Her son, who did the cooking, reacted faster than the retired constable who doubled as door-keeper and receptionist, racing up the stairs with a soiled white apron on and a butcher's boning-knife in his right hand.

His mother's whimpering drew him towards the scene of the tragedy, where he found her kneeling beside the corpse with her ample shoulders shaking. She pointed to the wound in the chest where a tell-tale patch of blood had escaped. No sort of coherent sounds came from her lips.

A travelling gent with a wide, greying, drooping moustache, boldly inserted himself in the doorway. The necessity to do something positive brought out the best in the plump youthful chef, who pressed a finger to his lips, and signalled for the curious one to wait outside.

He said: "*Por favor, señor.* The *Señor Haymes* has suffered a setback in the night."

The corpse compelled Fermina, the cleaner, to stare at the deceased again. Her mouth shaped up for another scream, but Alvaro, her son, firmly propelled her to the door and gave her into the charge of the salesman who had seen the inert figure without actually noticing the blood.

"*Señor*, please take my mother into the saloon next door. Ask Frisco, the barman, to give her a whiskey and also to send a message to the Boss, *Señor* Dorrance, who will need to be told."

The salesman clearly wanted to ask a whole lot of questions and do a bit of snooping on his own, but Alvaro's firmness prevented his so-doing. After hanging a *do not disturb* notice on the door of No. 1, the chef went below and whistled up a teenage boy, who was hastily despatched to summon the town marshal.

Pablo, the Mexican youth, pounded off down the street in his bare feet, his ragged white pants tight round his calf muscles. He had heard a few whispered exchanges about why the marshal was needed at the hotel and he knew his grandmother, Fermina, did not usually give way to her emotions.

Fifty yards along the street he pulled up, panting for breath, fanning his forehead with his straw hat. His dark rounded eyes lingered for a few seconds on the shingle above the peace office. It said: *Rudolph Girton, town marshal, Salt Creek City, Piute County, New Mexico territory. Knock and enter.*

No one ever did. At least, not first thing in the morning. Misdemeanours in Salt Creek tended to be of a minor nature, and long-term residents knew that their marshal had recently developed a drink problem, partly due to the lack of challenge in his job, and through boredom.

Pablo knocked. There were others beginning to show on the street, and many strollers were at once curious to know why anyone should want the marshal at such an hour.

"Hello, there! *Señor* Rudy! Can you hear me?"

Although he strained his ears at the substantial door, he could not detect any sort of a response. He called twice more, aware of the small crowd gathering in the street behind him. At last, he tried the door, found he could open it, and tiptoed inside. The room itself was spacious, dusty and in need of a good scrub out.

Light snoring drew his attention to the barred cells at the rear of the office. Marshal Rudy Girton was sleeping on the wooden shelf in the first cell, intended as furniture for confined customers.

Pablo crossed to the bars and urgently called the inmate, who interrupted his own snores, cautiously opened one bloodshot eye and hurriedly closed it again. Marshal Girton adjusted the position of his stubbled cheek against his dented black stetson, and mumbled:

"Something bothering you, Pablo?"

"*Si, si, Señor* Rudy! Alvaro sent me to fetch you to the hotel. Something has happened in Room No. 1. A man is dead, I believe! A visitor!"

Girton's eyelids showed definite signs of life, although they did not part.

"My grandmother needed whiskey, and someone has gone to summon *Señor* Dorrance. There will be more trouble if you don't come soon!"

Girton groaned. He knew he had a hangover, even before he shifted his head any distance. A slight feeling of panic was helping to clear his stupefied mind.

He was a long, lean sunbronzed fellow in his late twenties, with lush black curly hair and thin regular features. His green bandanna fitted him like a noose. His black shirt and trousers had seen better days. Only his

10

brown leather vest and the black scuffed riding-boots had been discarded before he turned in the previous evening.

He murmured: "Pablo, you wouldn't have the makings on you, would you? No, of course, you wouldn't. You don't smoke. Tell you what you'll do. Go right back, an' ask Blake, the door-keeper, to exclude anybody who is showin' too much curiosity. If Dorrance gets there before I do, put it around I'm already on the job, makin' enquiries. Okay?"

Yawning like a lion in agony, Girton slowly sat up and jerked to his feet. He picked up his crumpled hat, put it on and took it off because his head did not seem to like it any more. Pablo steadied him as he came out of the cell. The lad waited until he had successfully tipped water from a tall jug into a basin, and then he slipped away as swiftly as he had arrived.

Girton bathed himself with the tepid water and reflected on his recent luck.

Nothing to commend his uneventful term of office in the immediate past, and an ambitious mayor who had intimated that he would like to see a change of marshal when the next election was due. And who was the town mayor? None other than Jake Dorrance, the owner of the Salt Creek Hotel!

Five minutes later Girton elbowed his way through the swelling crowd which fronted the hotel, and danced up the staircase to prove how fit he was. He mastered his breathing so that others would not be able to comment how much out of condition he was, but there was a steady thumping of blood at his temples which reminded him of his drinking excesses of the night before.

The marshal entered No. 1 without hesitation and almost fell over a crouching figure by the bed. A rounded pair of shoulders supporting a shiny dark suit turned to face him. Doc Farrow's wild greying brown moustache and beard were a startling sight, even for his patients.

"Doc, you're here early," Girton remarked breathlessly.

As he talked, his restless brown eyes were regarding the body which had been raised and put upon the bed. He saw a paunchy figure with thinning greased hair and a scrawny neck. Silk pyjamas and a matching dressing-gown suggested affluence.

Girton sniffed, having detected the smell of hair-cream.

"If you didn't spend so much of your wages on strong liquor, Rudy, you could sure enough afford some of that fine-smellin' hair-oil."

Dr Herb Farrow straightened his rounded back and stepped away from the bed, making room for the peace officer. Girton nodded and moved closer, going down on one knee and taking a close look at the knife-wound in the chest. A clear case of murder was the only possible conclusion. The only death, apart from an accidental shooting or two since he had taken office. A dead man meant a lot of gossip, talk and unwanted publicity for a small town like Salt Creek. And a lot of pressure on the local peace office, not that it hadn't done an efficient job when the regular misdemeanours were of a simple nature.

"I sure am glad to see you on the job so early, Rudy," Farrow remarked, as he polished his spectacles on a coloured handkerchief. "'Cause our mutual friend, Jake Dorrance, sure as hell ain't goin' to like this, a murder in his hotel. In his best room, to boot!"

"Did you come across this hombre in your travels, Doc? I mean, did he ever seem to you like he might drum up an enemy in a town like this?"

Girton talked with an air of desperation. Already his throat was drying out again: fear was clouding his thoughts. He stood up rather

14

suddenly, suffered for it when his head thumped internally, and walked around the room, staring at this and that with an air of unreality.

"Nope. I don't rightly think he would. Make enemies, I mean. Inoffensive sort of fellow. Seeking his missing kin, as I heard tell. Ain't nothin' untoward about that. Don't look as if he found anything worthwhile either. Does it?"

Girton shook his head carefully. He wanted to ask the doctor if there was anyone in their community who had the instincts to stab a stranger to death in the best hotel, but already the medical man was packing his bag and edging towards the door.

"It's a mystery to me, Rudy. Get yourself abroad, start askin' questions. Look active. You don't have quite so many friends around the town as you used to do. It's my guess the killin' happened about midnight. If I'd stabbed this here fellow, I'd be miles away from town by now."

In the doorway the doctor hesitated. His watery eyes blinked a few times as he reflected upon what he had said. He added, "I guess," nodded several times, and left the building.

★ ★ ★

The smart buckboard pulled by the huge black gelding edged into the spot before the hotel just vacated by the doctor's conveyance. Less than five seconds had elapsed when Jacob Harold Dorrance sprang to the ground and hurriedly entered his establishment, answering the many polite "good mornings" with one curt nod.

Dorrance had been taken by surprise like everyone else when the unexpected message roused him from a comfortable bed a short distance out of town. Nevertheless, he had shaved and groomed himself before setting off for business.

At forty-five years of age his big shoulders were becoming weighty with flesh. His fancy shirt and grey cutaway coat hid more evidence of the good life around his waist and abdomen.

In spite of his bulk he was quiet on the stairs, and the first sound he made as he stepped into the murder-room was a gasp of surprise. Girton had drawn back the dividing curtain just prior to the hotelier's arrival. A fine big jug of cool water had been a temptation, as his head grew tired and his thoughts whirled. So he had stripped off his shirt and was in the act of leisurely bathing when Dorrance first caught sight of him.

Sheer bad feeling made the newcomer tear his attention away from the corpse to protest volubly. "Hell an' tarnation, Girton, just what are you up to? I hear tell of a murder in my hotel, in this very room, an' what do I find? The town's no-good peace officer in here bathin' himself as though nothin' had happened!"

Girton straightened up from the wash-basin, turned about and nodded politely. "Good day to you, Jake. I didn't expect you to be in town this early. I sure wish I had a job where I could delegate all my work to others an' turn up just when I fancied."

Dorrance lifted his big-brimmed grey hat and forcibly ran spatulate finger-tips through his long greying fair hair. "You won't have a job much longer, Girton!"

"Threatening a peace officer isn't the best way to begin a day," the marshal commented, "especially the sort of day this one is likely to be. The Doc's been an' the undertaker is on his way. I've talked briefly to some of your residents. Now, I'd like for you to go below an' see to it that all your staff are in the bar ready to be questioned by me in ten minutes!"

Dorrance chuckled ominously. "Now see here, I know you're boozed most of the time, but you surely recollect who is mayor of this town! I don't have to take any orders from you, Girton!"

"While you're rounding them up,

give thought to where you were last night, Mr Dorrance. All right? You an' a whole lot of other townsfolk will be questioned. Now, why don't you clear off an' give me another minute or two to look around. Do you like corpses?"

Warring emotions further unsettled the arrogant hotelier, who had been out of town consoling a rancher's wife who had been recently widowed. Haymes, the victim, did not mean a lot to him, but he found himself wondering if some enemy unknown had stabbed the poor fellow in his hotel to ruin his reputation as a hotelier.

He replaced his hat, and left the room.

★ ★ ★

An hour later Girton had done all the interrogating he intended at the hotel and retired to his office. There he mulled over his findings with Dixie Blake, the former constable, who now worked only as a receptionist. As he studied Blake across the top of his desk he found himself wondering if he was ever likely to end up looking the same way. At the time, the old fellow looked a mask of lush greying hair sprouting out of old discarded leather.

"A stranger," Girton intoned. "An' what does he amount to? A couple of valises. Some small change and a few dollars. Three suits, a photograph, shirts, underwear and a fine wig of golden hair, more suitable for a woman than a man."

"Anyone careless enough to flash that fancy money-belt around might put the law on the right trail, but otherwise his death will be forgotten in a matter of days. Only I don't think it will." Blake sighed heavily and absorbed himself by filling the bowl of his tobacco pipe.

"How so?" Girton enquired.

"Sort of chap to keep a murder fresh would be someone who wanted to disgrace the peace office. Like my new Boss, Jake Dorrance, who wants to

20

cut a dash as mayor an' looks forward to another marshal. One he can have in his pockets like that golden hunter watch of his."

Girton grunted. His stomach repeated sourly. He sprang to his feet and put a lot of strain on his swivel chair. Blake blinked a lot as the star-toting marshal headed for the door with his brown leather vest folded back.

* * *

In a little more than an hour Girton had talked to fifteen people. He had annoyed Jeanne-Marie Croissant, who ran a house manned by four young ladies who sometimes danced in the bigger saloons. None of them wanted to be questioned on account of the early hour, and they all were rude to him in turn, rejecting the idea that any of them would be likely to stab to death a potential client.

Two out of three boarding-house keepers had given him a bad time

21

for bothering their guests, and the otherwise friendly Mexican settlement in the adobes had been incensed, on account of his having spent several hours of the previous evening in their company drinking tequila.

Nevertheless, he had insisted on going through their *cantinas* and he had discovered a one-time drinking companion, Red O'Grady, who had turned nasty and refused to talk: with the result that Girton had been forced to root him out and march him off towards the peace office.

Fifty yards short of the office Red continued to mutter, his words sometimes coherent, other times not. Men lined up on either side of them, knowing that Girton and O'Grady had been close buddies at one time.

"What you takin' him in for, marshal?" a voice in the crowd asked.

"He's helpin' the peace office with enquiries," Girton explained breathlessly.

"Seems to me like one drunk accusin' another of murder," called another voice. "I don't reckon the marshal is in a fit state to answer questions about what *he* was doin' late on yesterday evenin'."

"Don't you put up with it, Red!" yet another advised.

Girton, who was tired, thirsty and far from happy, turned in the direction of the voice. Seconds later, Red's fist hit him behind the ear and dropped him heavily to his knees. Girton shook his head, hearing bells and seeing lights before the eyes. A circle of encouraging manhood formed about them, yelling for blood and action.

Red charged, but he was erratic. Girton stopped him with a solid straight-arm blow which landed under the chin, on the neck. O'Grady was suddenly short of the breath with which to protest. Stepping close, the marshal laid his .45 gun-barrel along the side of his head and caught him as he slumped.

Sensing the mood of the crowd, he fired his revolver into the air. The men backed off with every show of reluctance, and Girton was able to make it to his office door with the heavy frame over his shoulder. He could not recollect any time in his life when he felt more wretched.

2

AFTER a while, Red O'Grady slipped off into the sort of sleep from which he had been disturbed. The peace office went quiet and stayed that way. Dixie Blake went off on a tour of the liveries, seeking for information about fly-by-night visitors, or anyone who had quit town in a hurry, unnoticed.

Girton visited various places, and then stayed away, leaving the office manned by the bulky affable Mexican, Manuel Sanchez. No one disliked the formidable deputy. This was partly because he always grinned broadly in any sort of a tight situation, and partly because he had the blind courage of a lion. He could wrestle any man in town, hurting them or not hurting them as he thought fit.

Anyone asking pointed questions

about Girton received a big shrug of the beefy shoulders or a shake of the head which threatened to dislodge the wide drooping brown moustache which was Manuel's crowning feature.

Mayor Dorrance began to stir things up a little in the late afternoon by calling a meeting and chairing it himself, in the Salt Creek saloon next to his hotel. To get things moving and help the townsmen to see things his way, he sent his waiters in among them to offer a free drink, while he gave his views on the present troubling situation.

He stood with his chest thrown out, a lighted cigar in one hand and the thumb of his other hand stuck in a pocket of his waistcoat, the one in which he kept his watch.

"Friends, a town like this, a respectable settlement, with an unsolved murder, is a town in the shadow. I do not for a moment think that the murderer is in our midst. Why, we all know one another far too well to harbour a killer in our midst, and yet knowing a man lies dead in the undertaker's parlour is our responsibility."

"It's the town marshal's responsibility, mayor, not yours! That there Rudy Girton ain't the fellow he used to be when he first settled here after a spell in the cavalry. I don't think he's up to solvin' this killin' on his own!"

The speaker, a rancher with a thin mean face and a prominent Adam's apple, punctuated his talk by aiming a stogie like a dart. Dorrance found it hard to keep a smile off his face, because this character was saying all the things the hotelier wanted to hear without prompting. The other men at the nearest tables stamped the floor or called out their approval.

Dorrance held up his hand. "We mustn't be too hard on Marshal Girton. He has his problems, I guess."

More hoots of derision. More catcalls. More requests for the mayor to get on with his speech and spell it out, even if it did look bad for the marshal.

Dorrance obliged. He talked like a full-blown senator.

"I telegraphed the county seat over an hour ago. And do you know, the county sheriff knew nothing of this — this outrage in our town! Girton had omitted to inform them!"

The angry babbling which followed took a long time to level out. Those who wanted to know more were frustrated by others who merely wanted to hear the marshal's reputation rendered still blacker. In the middle of the uproar a stranger moved in through the batwings and painfully hobbled towards the nearest table. It was unoccupied, as it was far from the centre of interest. One or two men turned round to observe him: in time to notice how he pursed his lips, as though in pain from the left leg, which he dragged.

He was a tall, big-boned man with grey hair, worn long. A fine grey waxed beard stood out from his prominent chin, matched by a moustache which had been similarly treated. There was something which compelled attention in the newcomer. It had nothing to do with his fringed buckskin costume, nor the crudely-fashioned forked stick which he used as a crutch. It was something to do with the fierce hawk-like expression on the lined face which began in the grey penetrating eyes.

Dorrance paused in his tirade as the stranger slapped his big dusty flat-crowned hat on the table and hauled up another chair on which to rest his lamed leg. The hotelier blinked as he noted the twin holsters rigged in a crossdraw position at the stranger's waist.

"Don't mind me, folks," the newcomer murmured. "Just carry on. I don't want to interrupt anything of importance by intrudin' my presence." Dorrance nodded, bowed slightly, and resumed, but this time a lot of the fire and vitriol had gone out of his words. It was as if his purpose had turned sour on him. More and more of the townsmen were covertly showing interest in the buckskin stranger, so that the hotelier curtailed his speech, thanked his hearers for their attention and turned his own interest towards the newcomer.

"May I ask, sir, who you are, an' if you have any special interest in our town?"

The whole room seemed to sway as men leaned out of their chairs and peered. The newcomer grinned, in spite of himself.

"Well, all right then, if you're all so specially interested."

He fished in the pocket of his tunic and removed a five-pointed star which had seen better days. This, he pinned to the tunic pocket, taking great care.

"Ain't no reason for me to hide out none. My name is Sam Callaway. Federal Marshal of the United States. In the flesh. I'm here to renew acquaintance with a very old friend. Rudolph Girton, to be exact."

The silence which followed this revelation had a special quality to it. More and more men studied the direct grey-eyed stare, the rugged, wholly western features, and they wondered. Before he had arrived, they had been enjoying the slanging accusations against Rudy Girton to the full.

After a moment's hesitation Dorrance had another question to ask. "Did — did Girton ask you to come here, by any chance, marshal?"

"Not recently, no. But I owe him a visit. I'd like to think this town deserves Rudy Girton, folks. As likely as not the county sheriff didn't know about this little killin' hooha 'cause there's a county-wide hunt on right now for a bunch of hit-an'-run outlaws. I clashed with 'em myself. Picked up a bullet wound in the leg. I'll be around for a day or two, though, till my leg heals, so you'll get used to my ornery features."

Callaway chuckled. Dorrance called the meeting closed. His closest and hottest supporters deliberately dispersed so as not to be noted as likely conspirators against the town marshal.

The limping federal man lurched towards the bar, which opened again without any fuss. He started to regale himself with lukewarm beer, although his bullet-like eyes were studying the bottles of whiskey lined up against the long mirror.

Gradually, the men in the saloon began to act like normal. Some leaned on the bar. Others moved off with their drinks to tables far away from the long counter. Still more drifted towards the area where the green-baize topped card-tables were to be found. Conversations were guarded, and low. Many furtive glances were slanted in the federal man's direction.

The atmosphere was easy for a newcomer to read. Clearly, the town was in shock, following the murder. It was also clear that Dorrance was the presiding genius, and that he had an interest in the hotel. Callaway wondered what his background was, and why he was so bitter against Rudy Girton.

Presently, Frisco, the barman, began to make his presence felt. Frisco had spent a lot of time on the west coast, as his habitual nickname suggested. His experience of life was wider than that of many of his customers. His greased hair, parted down the middle, and his thin moustache and long tapering sideburns made him look like an eastern barber's shop tenor, but he had more intelligence than the drinkers usually gave him credit for.

In between trips up and down the bar he began to fill in little details about the high feelings against Girton for the benefit of Callaway. The federal man inclined his head and listened, soon having the impression that he was hearing the truth, simply delivered. He asked a few questions, as they occurred to him. Sometimes, he had to wait. Others, he received an immediate answer. Occasionally, he made do with a nod or a brief shake of the head, seen through the long mirror.

About a half-hour later Callaway thought he ought to withdraw. His non-stop toing and froing on horseback and on foot over the previous few days had given him an almighty thirst. On top of that, his wounded leg dragged. Either he had to pull out, real soon, or give way to a drinking-bout which might not do either Rudy Girton or himself any real good.

"You a friend of Girton's, Frisco?" The other sniffed, making his thin moustache ripple. "Yes an' no. I don't like to see him done down, like has been happening. All right, so he's taken to tippling. But this was a dull dead-an'-alive hole of a town before the murder. Me, I'd like to hit the bottle, too, only in my job it could prove fatal, one way or another. So I hope he gets lucky an' makes 'em all ashamed."

"You want to tell me where I can find him?" Frisco fished out of his pocket a piece of cardboard, on which he had calculated from time to time. In one corner he had written, *Go looking*

for Sally Bigelow, south-west of town.
Near the creek.

Callaway stuffed the card in his pocket. He thanked Frisco and promised to be in touch with him again. The horse on which he had arrived was little more than a cart-horse. Mounting it from the Indian side (the right) presented some slight difficulty, even with the crutch, but the federal man managed it.

3

SALLY BIGELOW had lived on the outskirts of Salt Creek City for over two years. Prior to that she had lived in a big modern house in San Francisco, as the wife of a rich man who owned several sea-going ships. Her husband had been married before, and when he was lost at sea, returning from a business trip to South America, his grown-up son and daughter and others connected with his first marriage had made life difficult for Sally. Consequently, she had left San Francisco for good, and turned her attention to the developing territories of the west, taking with her sufficient funds to allow her to set up house without having to become dependent upon another husband for cash.

The Bigelow house was a two-storey board building surrounded by a neat garden. A Japanese gardener and a smart coloured maid helped her with the work, indoors and out. Sally was friendly enough when she went into town shopping, but not many of the townsfolk were asked out to her residence. To pass away her spare time she did oil paintings and played her piano.

Just occasionally, someone went through who had known her on the coast, and then she went out of her way to make an old friend truly welcome. She cooked well and did not mind taking on much of the extra work which visitors caused herself.

Rudy Girton was one of the few townsmen who could arrive without warning and not be turned away. In recent months he had stayed away. He still cared for Sally, and he did not want to visit her in his present guise: that of a sorry peace officer, gripped by the need for regular intakes of strong liquor. A note delivered to the peace office by Geraldine, the little negress maid, had been instrumental in breaking his resolve to stay away from Sally, and it was to her house that he had gone when he felt the need to 'dry out' and straighten himself up in order to cope with the present emergency.

* * *

Sam Callaway's heavy-barrelled chestnut horse made the short ride to the Bigelow house seem a lot longer. It had been purchased from a farmer between towns shortly after the marshal's regular riding-horse had been shot dead under him.

He blinked appreciatively at the neat gardens, the painted shutters and the trees and flowers. Several windows were open, and the sound of voices carried to the rider as his mount made its plodding approach.

"Hey, Miss Sally, will you come an' see to this friend of yours? He's messin' around in the bath-tub, makin' a puddle on the carpet, so help me!"

From higher up in the building the owner's cultured voice answered. "You tell that no good town marshal I'll take the shotgun to him if he makes a mess in *my* house, Geraldine! You hear me?"

In spite of the ache in his wounded leg, Callaway was amused by the situation. He thought that Girton was getting all the attention that a man might expect in an expensive house of leisure, and no doubt getting it for free!

Callaway whistled: a high-pitched, disturbing whistle which caused his mount to do a lot of head-tossing and side-stepping.

A long-barrelled gun appeared round the end of a small greenhouse, its muzzle seeking out the newcomer and remaining steady on him. Callaway was impressed. He whistled once more, and this time Geraldine appeared round-eyed at one of the lower windows, while her mistress stuck her decorative head and shoulders through the window of an upper room.

From indoors came the sound of a man choking on an accidental intake of water. Then Girton coughed himself alive once more and made a loud-pitched "yippee" which suggested that the whistling meant something special to him.

"That you? That you, Sam Callaway?"

Girton's voice showed a lot more enthusiasm than when he had first arrived. He manipulated himself out of the ornate portable bath, wrapped himself in an expensive towel and tiptoed over the carpet to the nearest window, trailing soapy water.

Geraldine squawked in protest, and out of alarm. Callaway almost lost his balance as he dismounted, through laughing, and in a couple of minutes Sally, Geraldine and Sam were exchanging pleasantries, while Rudy rapidly towelled himself down in the next room and dressed in clean clothes.

Sally called for Tanaka, the youthful Japanese guard, to bring some drinks.

Callaway studied him appreciatively, knowing that his had been the hand which held the rifle by the greenhouse. The federal man also paid a lot of attention to his hostess.

Sally was a shapely woman in her late thirties, slightly above the average in height, with a long graceful neck, a becoming suntan and pale blue eyes. Her golden blonde hair was her best feature. At times she wore her tresses piled high on the top of her head, or combed out into an attractive bell around her shoulders. On this occasion she wore a pale blue headband which flattened the hair to her head around the forehead and temples, but let it fall free at the nape of her neck. Denims, a blue blouse and a darker blue apron completed her attire, and yet she moved nicely, and her shape still remained alluring.

Although the house was normally free from smoke, Sally encouraged these two old friends to light up a couple of small cigars, along with their whiskey. She seated herself in a high-backed chair, shooed Geraldine off to the kitchen, and listened politely.

"Sam, I have to ask you. Were you on your way to look me up when you absorbed that bullet-hole in the leg?" Girton asked eagerly.

"Well, yes an' no, Rudy. I was ridin' along, hopin' to make contact with a bunch of outlaws who'd committed a couple of federal offences, an' at the same time lookin' forward to seein' you. I'm still real pleased to see you, even though you have trouble in town, an' I have a slight hole in the leg. Maybe we can help each other. What do you think, Sally?"

The blonde smiled, showing good teeth, and glanced from one of them to the other. "I think the two of you could help each other. Rudy has gotten himself into a rut. He could do to clear town for a while, do some ridin' — like he used to do with the cavalry. Freshen his image a little, an' maybe seek for a murderer who has already left.

"As for you, Mr Callaway, you surely need a week or two out of the saddle. Perhaps you could do to take a desk job till your leg is mended."

Callaway chuckled. "That sure does seem like a really profitable scheme, Sally. I'll go along with that. Take over from Rudy for a while, if no one in town objects. What do you say, old friend?"

"I think it would work," Rudy admitted, "only I'll have to wait until the burial. That is, if there's goin' to be a burial. I don't suppose anyone had telegraphed or anything, about poor Wilbur Haymes' death?"

"Nothing at all that I heard on, Rudy. Maybe the two of us could attend the plantin', if there's nobody showin' any special interest. Every now an' again a strange face shows up at a burial. That way, you could get a lead of sorts."

Sally topped up the glasses with more liquor. "I can't help wondering where you'll start looking, if there are no leads at all in town, Rudy."

Callaway adjusted the position of his injured leg and waved his cigar. "If Sally doesn't mind hearing a lot more talk, I'd like to hear a few more details, Rudy."

Rudy emptied his glass, studied it for a moment, and decided to use a little will power and refuse a refill. His friends noted this, and each of them was quietly pleased.

"It seems there was a strike against a train by an outlaw gang. A year or two ago. Further over than Piute Junction. Nearer the Texas border. My corpse, Wilbur Haymes, was in a part of the train disconnected from the locomotive an' the mail-van an' such. As a result, when some jasper used too much dynamite in order to force an entry to the valuables, the rest of Haymes' family disappeared. The explosion blew most of the mail-van apart, and also set fire to the passenger carriage immediately behind it, in which the family were.

"Since then, Haymes hasn't been in touch with his folks. In fact, he's missed the chance altogether, now he's dead. Maybe if I continued his search, I'd find out how he came to be killed."

Rudy had talked with gathering excitement. He became suddenly thoughtful, and his listeners wondered what it was which had just occurred to him. To give him a breathing-space, Sam added a bit of information of his own.

"If my information is correct, the gang I've just been tanglin' with, known as the Border gang, were the same bunch of hombres who attacked that train you just spoke of. So maybe there's a tie-up between your business an' mine. But I thought you were goin' to add something."

Rudy frowned thoughtfully, and then shook his head. "I don't know, really." He stared at Sally, who blushed and felt over her hair. "Sally, this poor galoot, Haymes, had a fine wig of long soft blonde hair. Not so golden as yours. What I can't figure out is, why did he have such a thing? Do you have any ideas?"

After assuring Sam that her hair was real, Sally behaved more seriously. "If it was intended for a woman, I suppose he meant it as a present. Assumin' that he was only interested in his own kin, it would have to be for his wife, or possibly his daughter. Did he have a daughter?"

Rudy nodded. "Sure, I believe he has a daughter an' a son, as well as the missin' wife. I guess it could have been an intended gift. Here's another thing. Assumin' mother, daughter an' son all escaped that fire an' blast without any serious injury, where are they now? An' why haven't they made some sort of a move to rejoin Haymes? Was he some sort of a tyrant, or do all three of them have some other reason for stayin' away?"

"It's possible they're bein' kept out of circulation," Sam remarked mildly.

"You think they may be held as

hostages? Something like that, Sam?"

Callaway shrugged. "The passage of time makes it seem unlikely, but we have to start reasonin' somewheres, that's for sure."

Sally pressed a long slim finger to her lips. It was her turn to be pensive. The two smoking men were both aware of her silence. They waited for her to explain.

"For what it's worth, Rudy, there's only one store where a man could buy a head of false hair like that," she began. "Always assuming that Haymes bought it in Piute County an' not somewhere over the Texas border. The store in question is located in North Creek. If you're intent on riding around asking questions, North Creek might be worth a visit. I'm sure the proprietor of the store would remember your man, if he shopped there."

Rudy ground out his cigar into an ornate metal ashtray. He nodded slowly, but without showing any marked confidence in Sally's suggestion.

After a pause, he said: "Is there much of a sale in this neck of the woods for false hair, Sally?"

Sally sat forward. She crossed and uncrossed her elegant legs before replying. "Well, now, I wouldn't rightly know the answer to that one, peace officer. You sure enough will have to ask the shop proprietor, won't you? I can assure you, though, he does have a stock of such items, luxury goods or no luxury goods.

"And they aren't cheap. Someone has to assemble a good head of hair from a human head. They aren't scalps, you know. All that hair has to be grown, and grown in the natural way. But if I put you off by mentioning the wig shop, I'm sorry."

Rudy rose to his feet, beaming and waving his hands in a placating fashion. "No, no, no. I didn't want to give that impression. I appreciate your lively interest in me an' my problems, Sally. Just the same as I value Sam's advice and presence. Tomorrow, sometime,

48

I'll definitely leave town an' take in this wig shop in North Creek.

"Up until Sam arrived, I wasn't feelin' all that interested in the Haymes affair. Now, I find I may be on the trail of a missin' family who could possibly do with a friendly bit of help, an' my interest has grown. I don't feel depressed any more about the prospect of being voted out of office as a peace officer, come the next election."

Sally clapped briefly. Sam banged his heels on the floor and flinched on account of his wound. It was his turn to bathe.

4

THE burial of Wilbur T. Haymes was carried out without incident in the town's burial ground shortly before eleven a.m. the following morning. The hotelier was there, a couple of ranchers who had contrived to be in town for the event, a newspaper proprietor from North Creek and some twenty or thirty hangers-on of no regular employment.

Side by side, Rudolph Girton and Sam Callaway surveyed those who made the trek from the church to Boot Hill, but neither of them spotted anyone acting in the kind of fashion that a guilty murderer at times adopted.

The parson talked for quite a while, even though he knew very little of Haymes' life and business before he arrived in the town, and by the time the coffin had been lowered all the onlookers were as thirsty as the undertaker and the parson.

Callaway had borrowed for the journey a buckboard, and Rudy shared it with him. From time to time the two peace officers were the focus of close scrutinies, but they had become immune to open staring, and they only had to glare purposefully back at any persistent offenders for the others to back down.

As an investigator, Girton was something of an unknown quantity: Callaway was even more so, but already the word had gone around that the veteran star toter was staying in town indefinitely, and that had an effect upon many of the townsmen. Most westerners did not like answering personal questions at any time, but on this occasion when a murder was causing the stir many of them backed off at the earliest opportunity, using as an excuse urgent business.

Sam and Rudy talked briefly with the parson and the undertaker. The buckboard and its load was away early. Already Rudy had made arrangements for Pablo, the Mexican boy, to collect his dun horse from the West End Stable. Much as Girton enjoyed the company of his old comrade and riding partner, he was anxious to be on his way. He wanted to restore himself to his old standard of fitness through riding, exercise and success in his work. Only that way could he feel again the kind of self-esteem which had motivated him when he first became a peace officer.

Sam knew what was griping him. They took one large whiskey apiece in the bar adjacent to the hotel, and talked over one or two aspects of the murder and that other business of the rampaging outlaw gang known as the Border boys.

Ten minutes short of noon Rudy mounted up, shook hands with his old friend and walked his excited dun horse clear of town to westward, prior to turning north. Gradually, the traffic on the dusty northbound trail thinned out, and the lone rider lost interest in those who might be coming towards him from the opposite direction.

A hot dusty trail had the effect of dulling a riding man's ardour in a very short time. He found himself thinking that apart from Sam and Sally he had few really serious friendships back there in Salt Creek City. Some men in his shoes with no particular ties might have simply ridden away and kept on riding, seeking another spot — more attractive than the last — in which to put down his roots . . .

He shrugged away such negative thoughts and concentrated upon the undulating trail. The dun was soon sweating, being slightly out of condition for a protracted ride. Rudy leaned forward, talking encouragingly to it and lightly massaging the white blaze forward of its ears. He had ridden far enough to know that he still had in him a touch of the wanderlust.

The time passed slowly. The sun

appeared to drag itself across the heavens with monotonous lack of effort. Soon, his green bandanna had turned a deeper shade through perspiration and his black shirt developed a damp patch between the shoulder-blades.

Will power kept him from sleeping for several punishing miles, and then he dozed. The dun was quite used to such a happening. He was not likely to slip out of the saddle, but progress with the rider in that state meant careful plodding by the horse.

Towards three in the afternoon the horse struck sparks from small track stones and then boosted the hunched rider back to full consciousness. He liked the look of the grass and scrub behind the trailside rocks to his right and that helped him to a diversion.

He turned the dun off-trail, found a small park where tall standing rocks afforded shade, and there swung out of leather. The dun snorted with pleasure, especially when he slackened the saddle and stripped out all the harness down to the blanket. There was no trickling water near the park, but the short grass had a lush greenness to it which suited the animal well.

Within a few minutes Girton was sleeping soundly with his head resting upon his saddle and his dented hat shading his face.

★ ★ ★

One hour later he was on the move again. On they went for another two hours, riding down onto the smoking mixed township of North Creek a little after six in the evening. The slanting rays of the westering sun came lancing right at them until the first of the log and board buildings afforded them a welcome shade.

Rudy decided to take down his marshal's star before anyone in this new community got used to seeing it. He then found for himself a small clean lodging-house on the outskirts of town where he could clean up, have the promise of an evening meal and the assurance of a bed. The dun was awarded similar treatment at the east end of town.

Having been under the pump and changed his shirt, Rudy found himself drawn to the emporium which bore the name of Clint Church's Western Arcade. It had no less than three street entrances, having a broad front. There were serving counters in from each door. The stock-rooms and offices were further to the rear.

Rare luxury goods hung from the board ceiling like mobile ornaments, while tailors' dummies and east coast display units cluttered up the floor in places. Under the counters were glass display cases, while the side and rear walls were full of creaking shelves loaded with boxes, cartons and bales of all descriptions.

At one end, an elderly clerk in a dark suit was in charge. The counter in the middle was unmanned, but at the other end was a youthful attendant with bright red hair and a long neck. The latter came from behind his barrier and beamed, his smile splitting his hairless face from one protruding ear to the other.

"Good day to you, sir. Can I help you?"

Rudy nodded and smiled. "If it ain't too much trouble I'd like to speak to the proprietor for a moment or two. Could that be arranged?"

The redhead looked very startled and peered past the customer to the other end of the room where the elderly assistant affected a total lack of interest and merely shrugged his shoulders in reply to the unspoken query.

"Is Mr Church in the building?" Rudy persisted gently.

The redhead nodded and glanced in the direction of a door behind the centre counter. "Yes, sir, he surely is, but he doesn't really take part in the running of the shop after six in the evening."

"My business is of a serious nature, young man."

The lad gulped and nodded, and approached the door almost on tiptoe. The door in question opened and closed behind the boy. A minute later he was back again, his breath returning to normal respiration. Rudy was wondering what sort of an interview he was in for when the door opened once again and into the room swept a tall, lean theatrical figure with a commanding presence.

Clinton Church had been an actor of sorts for many years in some of the states down the eastern seaboard. Mostly around New York, Philadelphia and Delaware. He had a full head of fine silver-grey hair, topped by a small black skullcap, and an imposing set of facial whiskers of a darker shade. His moustache, beard and sideburns were carefully trimmed every morning of his life.

"What can I do for you, my friend?" The timbre of the voice denied the man's sixty years. He undid the magnificent red and green silk dressing-gown which hid his waistcoat and most of his tailored trousers, set it in place again, and fixed his dangling monocle in his right eye. He did not seem to find anything to excite him in Girton's appearance.

"I'm sorry to trouble you, Mr Church. My name is Girton. I am the town marshal of Salt Creek City. Enquiries connected with a recent sudden death in my town bring me here. I wonder if we could speak in private for a few moments?"

Church became more businesslike. He gestured to his assistants to carry on with whatever they were doing and himself led the way to the door by which he had entered. Through it, Rudy found himself in a small sitting-room, tastefully laid out with a three-piece, mirrors, paintings and a couple of expensive lamps.

Church indicated a box of cigars on a low table, and seemed mildly surprised when Rudy took one and lighted it for himself. Only then did the marshal take off his hat and remove from it the fine blonde wig which had been found in Wilbur Haymes's room.

"Could you tell me anything about this wig, sir?"

Church took it and draped it across his knees. He polished his eye-glass thoroughly before taking a closer look at the hair-piece, and then he relaxed.

"Fine hair," he murmured, "taken from a young woman of good breeding and probably intended for another young woman who wanted to look a little different from her usual self. How does it tie in with the death?"

Rudy savoured the taste of his cigar smoke. "It was found among the belongings of a travelling gent, name of Wilbur Haymes. I wondered if by any chance he had bought it from you, an' whether you knew him. Right now, I'm tryin' to find out about his contacts in the area, an' I don't have a lot to go on. He died suddenly, of a knife wound.

Probably killed because he startled an intruder, a thief. But I'd dearly like to be put in touch with any of his kin, because it's clear by what the townsfolk of Salt Creek knew of him he was on the lookout for his missing family."

"I believe this wig might have been purchased in my shop, but I can't really tell you anything about the purchaser," Church answered, shaking his head.

Rudy showed him the old print, and this time he studied the photograph without the benefit of the glass lens. The group was a clear one. Seated was the woman believed to be Haymes' wife. Behind her was Haymes himself, while the son and daughter were one on either side, standing.

Mrs Haymes' hair was fixed in two buns, one over each ear. It looked to be quite long, and light in colour. The daughter's long hair appeared to be slightly longer, parted centrally and allowed to fall over either shoulder, without benefit of clips or slides.

The daughter resembled her mother,

but the tall, dark-haired, bright-eyed young man with the hairline moustache bore little resemblance to his father. Rudy found himself noting for the first time that Haymes appeared to be a good few years older than his wife. Was it possible he had been the woman's second husband? Was he only stepfather to her grown-up children? The young peace officer found himself trying to see this group as they might be when not posing for a photographer. He was in a sort of reverie when Church cleared his throat, and disturbed his thoughts.

"Such a pity I'm not able to help you more, marshal," the proprietor remarked, his voice conveying regret.

"You don't think it's any use asking your two assistants if they have any recollections of that wig sale?"

Church blustered, blowing out his formidable moustache. "No. No, marshal. Not really. You see, my elderly assistant is very short-sighed, an' the other fellow hasn't been with us very long. So it wouldn't help. Where will you look next?"

Rudy sniffed. "You have the look of a gracious man, Mr Church. I feel sure you will give me the benefit of your expert advice."

The marshal leaned forward, expectantly. Church shuffled in his seat, as though he was forced to volunteer information against his will. He toyed with his monocle, and worked his eyebrows up and down a few times.

"I guess women wear wigs for vanity," he opined, after a pause. "Occasionally, people wear them as a disguise, to pass themselves off as something different. On the stage, in the theatres, they are frequently used. You even get drag artists wearing them at times."

"Drag artists, Mr Church? Could you explain that to me?"

"A male actor in drag wears the make-up and clothes of a woman, marshal. There was a time when only men graced the boards. Now, we have both sexes. In some music halls a man dressed as a female often has a special attraction."

"But in western theatres, some of them little more than barns," Rudy persisted. "Surely we don't have drag artists in these parts?"

Clinton Church waved a deprecating hand. "Oh yes we have," he argued. "There's a series of travelling turns working their way round Piute County at this very minute. If I'm not mistaken, one particular act is a twosome. Two men, who travel around together. Why don't you find out where they are? One of them might know a whole lot more about wigs than *I* do! Your enquiry might just pay off!"

The interview was suddenly concluded. As Rudy could not think of any other questions to ask, he shook the owner by the hand and allowed himself to be escorted into the street. For a moment he hesitated, undecided what to do next. Men walked slowly past him, staring at the wig hanging from his left hand. He flinched, recovered his self-possession, and restored the hair-piece to its former hiding-place.

He was still frowning when he reached his lodging-house. The idea of a man in drag being involved in Haymes' demise intrigued him, but even so he could not imagine such a fellow leaving a wig at the scene of the crime. Nevertheless, he intended to make contact with the drag artist, if at all possible.

His landlady gave him a meal of substantial, stodgy food, which he digested without much difficulty. After that, he began a walk-about, wandering around the places of entertainment, wondering where his sort of information could be picked up.

In a saloon called the Creek Cascade, which appeared to have an excess of beer spilled into its sawdust carpet, he inserted his lean form so that he could see the upright piano and the white man with the blackened face who was singing by it. Shortly after he entered the building the singing and playing stopped. The applause was only lukewarm, and the entertainers took a breather. After sinking a few fingers of whiskey at the bar Rudy moved over to their table to talk to them.

As he did so two men who had been seated on a low wooden bench against a wall — not far from the batwings — began to take a special interest in him. They were the brothers McCade, Jay and Cal, two small-time crooks who did not care for work, and who bummed a living by preying on their fellow men in one way or another.

Six months previously Girton had arrested the pair of them for mugging a drunk one Saturday evening on a dark night in Salt Creek. Cal was more observant than his brother, who had a slight squint. He tilted his beer glass and tipped the last of his drink through the brown bewhiskered opening which was his mouth.

"Say, Jay, will you take a look at that fellow over there. The one talkin' to the piano player. Ain't that Rudy Girton, the town marshal of Salt Creek?"

Jay, who had already drained his glass, blinked his close-set eyes and peered towards the upright piano. "Hell an' tarnation, Cal, I do believe you're right! It's the guy who locked us up for a couple of days an' took all our savings as a fine! What's more, he's out of his territory, an' he ain't wearin' no peace officer's badge. Are you thinkin' what I'm thinkin', brother?"

They were in their early thirties: swarthy, slightly overweight, unshaven and generally unkempt. Cal slumped towards his brother, massaging the rounded profile of his Roman nose with a calloused forefinger. He began to snigger. Jay did the same. It was a family failing. The batwings swung open, and a very sober-looking farmer stepped inside. Cal nudged his brother, rose to his feet and casually moved closer to the newcomer.

"Say, friend, if you're goin' over there towards the bar, would you do a small favour for me?"

The farmer shrugged, gave a guarded smile, and was prepared to listen.

"I want you to go over to that hombre speakin' to the pianist. Tell him an old friend is waitin' for him on the sidewalk. With information which he may be looking for. All right?"

The farmer seemed doubtful. He massaged his chin and thought about his thirst. "Could be worth a couple of whiskeys when he gets back inside," Cal coaxed.

Patting him on the shoulder, the farmer shrugged again, and moved off in the direction of Girton who was not making any progress, and yet was enjoying his conversation. Cal tugged urgently at his brother's sleeve. When the farmer had almost made it as far as the piano, he turned to glance back at them, but they were already outside.

Cal went one way and Jay went the other. They were adept at blending into whatever cover presented itself. Partially hidden by uprights which supported the sidewalk, they waited for Girton to emerge, and at the same time kept a sharp watch on the walking traffic in the vicinity.

Girton came out quickly. He glanced about him, eager to make contact with an old friend. Especially one who could give him the sort of information he was looking for. A man stood about three yards away with his back to the batwings, crouched over, lighting a cigarette.

"Over here, Rudy," the smoker murmured.

Girton approached him. Behind him, Jay McCade matched his footsteps as he crept up silently. As the smoker straightened up, Rudy felt his first intimation of suspicion. Instinct warned him of the man at his rear. He paused, side-stepped and was in time to avoid Jay's sneak attack. An elbow sank deep into the squinting man's fleshy midriff.

Jay staggered, and Cal found his right swing blocked in mid-air. Rudy was alerted by now. He traded punches with Cal, while Jay fought to recover his breath. Cal began to slow down, being out of condition for a fair fight. Jay managed to land a glancing blow on Girton's head, but he was wary of the marshal's flying fists and withdrew out of distance as Rudy shifted his attention.

The marshal took out Cal with a weighty backhanded swing, which caught his adversary in the throat and made him gag for air as he sank to the boards. The nearest strollers were no more than twenty yards away, and yet the action was uninterrupted.

Rudy grappled with Jay as the latter rushed him with his head down. He swung the charging man round, using his momentum to put him off-balance. The McCade survivor had his back to the wall, and was being measured for a knockdown blow when the unexpected happened.

The farmer had emerged again and, thinking that he owed some sort of loyalty to the brothers, he pulled a gun and clouted Girton across the back of the head with it. Girton sighed gently and sank to his knees, collapsing forward. The farmer stepped back, chuckling to himself. The fallen McCade slowly picked himself up. A group of liquored men surged out of the batwings, causing the brothers to look disinterested.

When they moved on, the farmer grew more bold. "Hey, you two, don't you think you owe me a few fingers of whiskey, seein' as how your old buddy turned difficult? I figure you owe me something. I didn't have to alert him, now, did I?"

He returned his Colt to its holster with loving care. Further up the street a constable carrying a lighted lamp in one hand and a shotgun in the other came slowly but inevitably nearer. The brothers exchanged whispers, starting away down the sidewalk in the opposite direction to the peace officer.

"Hey, hold on!" the farmer protested.

"You hold on, *amigo*, if you want

the constable to find out you just slugged a town marshal!" Cal advised.

The farmer gasped and retreated indoors. Girton's hat gently disengaged itself from his head and tipped over, spilling the blonde wig onto the boards where a pool of muddied spilled beer caused its condition to deteriorate.

5

BY the time the constable arrived on the scene the sidewalk was empty, except for Rudy Girton's crumpled body.

"You all right there, boy?"

Constable Smoky Nelson was a fifty-six-year-old with a grey walrus moustache, who in recent years was never far from his shotgun. He scarcely ever fired it, but toting it around gave men the impression that he knew how to use it and that he would not hesitate if pressed to do so.

"Hold, hold on a minute, will you?" Girton mumbled, his head still not clear.

Rudy's groping hand came upon his hat, and then the matted blonde wig. Feeling it under his hand, and knowing what it was, helped his head. He blinked hard and slowly rose to his feet. Behind him, Nelson chuckled.

"That there forty rod served in the Cascade sure is potent these days. You should have been warned."

Rudy sniffed, and leaned against the wall. "My condition doesn't have anything to do with the watered whiskey," he remarked bleakly. "I was called out on a faked message, an' struck from behind by a third man, after dealin' with the first two. If you'd happened along sooner, you could've helped."

"You're amakin' a lot out of a very minor deal it seems to me," Nelson replied, without warmth.

Rudy fumbled in his pocket. "You know what this is?" He showed his marshal's star. "Now, take me along to the peace office. I figure this town owes me something, an' I aim to ask your man a few questions."

Nelson shrugged. He shifted the lamp across to the same side as the shotgun, and grudgingly supported Girton, who made his way on faltering legs, until

74

the peace office was reached.

Rudy's head was spinning again as they went in. He slumped down in an upright chair and lowered his head between his knees. His lungs were filling with stale air and pungent cigar smoke, as he strove to regain control of himself.

The big chair behind the desk creaked. "You picked up another drunk already, Smoky?"

Without looking up, Rudy remarked: "You have any reward dodgers for a couple of brothers who specialize in mugging an' robbing selected victims?"

Marshal Russ Blades was a bulky forty-year-old; bald headed, with a sandy moustache and sideburns. The habitual scowl located around his jutting chin and protruding underlip deepened.

"Who is 'e, Smoky?"

"Claims he's a town marshal, like yourself, Boss. Showed me a badge. I guess he knows best."

"Rudolph Girton, marshal of Salt

Creek. First time in your town for over a year, an' jumped by the brothers McCade. I put them away for similar tricks about six months ago. Have you encountered them?"

Blades lowered his newspaper, blinked in Nelson's direction and folded his arms. He was a one cigar a day man, and he did not like visitors while he was actually smoking that one. He rolled the half-smoked cigar around his mouth expertly.

"Well, howdy, Girton. Sorry you got caught up in old business. Can't say I've ever heard of the McCades. Sure enough, they ain't ever jumped me."

Blades chuckled, and Nelson added some husky laughter, after carefully discarding his shotgun. At that moment Rudy's head cleared again. He fixed the pair of them, one at a time, with a sharp glare of appraisal.

"What can you tell me about Clint Church? Is he honest, above-board?"

"Now see here, Girton, you ain't startin' to investigate North Creek more solid citizens, are you?" Blades protested. "Why shouldn't he be honest an' above-board?"

Rudy shook his head, unable to answer that one. As he did so, he felt dizzy again. He was not pleased when his opposite number chuckled again and drew attention to his face.

"Say, Girton, you're sufferin' more than I thought. Right at this minute you have mud or somethin' runnin' down the side of your face, out from under your hat-brim!"

Rudy groaned. When he had been struggling to recover his senses he had stuffed the sullied wig on his head, under his stetson. Now, he knew what Blades was talking about. He took off his soiled black hat and extracted the once glamorous blonde wig, glaring at it with mixed feelings.

Smoky Nelson showed surprise. "Hey, Mr Girton, you ain't been scalpin' some pretty girl on your travels, have you? That there sure enough looks like a woman's hair, don't it?"

Blades' chair creaked as he strained for a better look.

"It's a bought wig," Rudy explained. "That's what I went to see Church about. There's a connection with a man murdered in Salt Creek a few days back. I'm lookin' for his missin' kin, like he was when he was stabbed. Don't suppose you've encountered two women an' a young man usin' the name of Haymes?"

His query received a negative shaking of heads. He asked permission to rinse the hair-piece in a wash-hand basin and received it from his curious listeners. As he was doing the rinse, he talked.

"I heard tell that entertainers sometimes use wigs like this. I was wonderin' if you had heard about travellin' players who dress up. Maybe men who dress up as women. Did you ever hear anything? Anything of that in town recently?"

Blades shook his head very decidedly, but Nelson was more impressed. Prompted by Rudy, the constable raked about in his memory, and then nodded heavily.

"We did have entertainers in the county a short while ago. I heard there was a couple of fellows doin' an unusual act. One was a dame comedian, or a female impersonator, if I have his title right. Does that help?"

Rudy carefully lifted the wig out of the bowl and squeezed it with great care. "It could help if you could tell me where to look for them!"

Nelson glanced at Blades for guidance. The latter did tricks with the last inch of his cigar, and shrugged his shoulders.

"I did hear tell they was headed for North Creek, then something went wrong with their arrangements, so they turned around an' headed for Saguaro. Just a few days ago, so help me."

Rudy began to feel better. His head had cleared. He was being given a lead, of sorts. He was about to voice his thanks when the street door opened under pressure, and two young farmers came in, supporting an elderly man whose shirt and jacket were torn. Blood and a bruise disfigured his face.

"It ain't safe in this burg no more," the injured man complained. "Caught me between one lighted building an' another, they did. Heavy, shifty-eyed jaspers with beards . . . "

"Jay an' Cal McCade, I'll be bound," Rudy remarked lightly. "Shifty-eyed is right. One squints, the other has a Roman nose."

Girton backed off, quietly pleased — in a way — at this development. Blades demanded to know where the attack had taken place, and how long ago. He ordered his man to hurry to the liveries at one end of the town while he, himself, hotfooted it for the other.

"A word of advice, marshal," Rudy offered, before the two men had left the office. "The brothers McCade don't usually hightail it out of town. Their usual dodge is to horn in on a gamblin' game, an' make-believe they've been there for hours."

Marshal and constable hesitated for a few seconds, while the injured man and his supporters studied Girton with eyebrows raised. Rudy stepped through them all, casually called out his thanks, and made it onto the street ahead of all opposition. Although he had made a mental note to sort out the McCades some time soon, he had no intention of getting involved in this night's latest caper. He headed for his lodgings.

* * *

Saguaro had been named about forty years previously when wandering boundary stretchers happened upon it, and remarked upon several huge stands of tall cactus of the saguaro variety, which invariably stood up from the dry soil like a giant's hand reaching for the sky.

It was a small, mixed community. Apart from a few farms in the vicinity, plus a ranch or two, all it had to commend it and ensure its continuing prosperity was a useful, busy telegraph line.

Rudy Girton started out on horseback late that morning, having celebrated his short stay in North Creek by absorbing a few fingers of whiskey to deepen his sleep. He awoke a couple of hours after daybreak with a slight headache, and a feeling that he had over-indulged himself.

However, his conscience did not trouble him for long. He ran out the dun horse, which was also a little out of training, and headed west in the middle of the morning. The dehydrating heat of the sun made him rest off-trail in the afternoon, with the result that he did not actually ride into Saguaro until early evening.

The town was quiet. Quieter than ordinary. The reason had to do with the entertainment taking place in the huge, lofty barn reserved for special occasions and travelling players. He left his mount at the hitch-rail this time, and hurried into the barn, paying half the usual entrance fee as the turns had almost finished.

To his delight he found that the one turn he was really interested in was on stage. The turn consisted of two troupers, billed as Lolita and Leopoldo. Lolita was dressed as a full-bodied Mexican woman in a short gaudy skirt, a straining bra and a tight red bolero. A huge floppy sombrero topped the grotesque figure and partially hid the long black hair which hung over the powerful shoulders.

Lolita had a husky voice, and did most of the leading when it came to juggling with Indian clubs and conjuring with cards and coloured silk handkerchiefs. The more youthful partner, who was in his middle twenties, had the figure of a Spanish bullfighter and the pale impassive face often associated with a successful toreador.

The piano played, and Lolita sang. Leopoldo mouthed the words and smiled, but never uttered a sound, which led Girton to believe that he might have some sort of a speech defect.

As the climax to the act, Lolita and Leopoldo faked a quarrel, after which the formidable Lolita chased her man all over the stage, diving over him and occasionally through his legs, until at last they clashed together and flopped on their buttocks to the accompaniment of loud clapping and boot stamping.

Encouraged by the pianist, they took three bows, at the end of which Lolita discarded her bolero and ran across the stage in skirt and bra. To renewed applause the bra itself was held in view from the wings, before the two of them reappeared and bowed for the last time.

Then, and only then, it became clear that Lolita was a well-built fellow in early middle age, dressed in female drag costume.

The audience goggled and cheered. Rudy gave his full attention to the pair, although his interest was a little more professional than critical. He stepped aside as the townsfolk who had seen all the acts trooped out of doors, and returned to their homes, or in search of liquid nourishment.

Suddenly, the new arrival felt depressed. What had he hoped to learn from such an outfit as that? Only one of the pair wore a wig, and Lolita's use of the false hair had been merely to render more amusing a comic act.

He walked the streets, after surrendering his horse to a livery, looking in at the lighted windows of eating-shops, wondering about the missing Haymes woman and her daughter. Surely Leopoldo couldn't have anything to do with that missing son, shown in Haymes' photograph.

Rudy grimaced as he tried to compare what he had seen in the indifferent light of the stage with the far-from-distinct features in Haymes' family group.

He found himself feeling tired, hungry and frustrated. The riding had not been as punishing as on the journey from North Creek, but he was still far from his old fitness as a cavalryman.

After a meal, in the privacy of his room, he studied again the photograph and admired the woman's hairpiece which had responded to his efforts to wash it and comb it out again. The wig was hanging on the end of his bed when he attempted to sleep.

And once again, sleep was far from easy. This time he stayed alert through trying to visualize the Haymes girl wearing the false tresses. The shadowy image of a fleet-footed girl stayed with him in a dream which aroused him long before daylight. After that he projected his thoughts back to Sam Callaway and Sally Bigelow until his eyelids grew exceedingly heavy and closed him out for several hours more.

His waking thoughts were punctured by a vision of Sam Callaway charging into battle on horseback, riding against several masked outlaws with a single long weapon which was sometimes a rifle and other times a wooden crutch.

6

THE powerful sun was laying claim to a place in the sky long before Girton awoke the following morning. He lay on his back, savouring the smell of coffee drifting up from the street through his open window. He thought that the west, although vast in extent, was unique in its smells.

Presently, his mouth filled with saliva. He rose, poured water in his basin, and prepared himself for another day. As he worked on himself, his thoughts went back to Salt Creek. He wondered how Sam Callaway was making out, and whether that troublesome leg wound was still painful.

Somewhere in Piute County an outlaw gang was skulking. It occurred to him that he had not shown a great deal of interest in Sam's pressing problems, on account of his own anxiety about Wilbur Haymes. There were many small communities north of the rail-road line in the terrain he had ridden into. Where, he wondered, were those Border outlaws at this time?

Five minutes later he went downstairs and started his breakfast. An impassive landlady with a bronze sheen to her skin served him with plenty of well-cooked food and asked him no questions.

Soon, he was out on the street and making his way in the direction of the barn. No one challenged him, or asked who he might be. In the barn itself a whistling old man with white spreading whiskers informed him that all the travelling players had shown restlessness the night before.

Either they had moved out before nightfall, or they had started on their travels on the right side of breakfast-time.

Rudy scratched his head, and sniffed disconsolately. "So what sort of lodgings did they go for in town, *amigo*?"

"Mostly, travellin' theatrical folks keep themselves to themselves. They come in their own wagons. Park 'em by water, or the iron way, an' move out just as it suits them. Ain't but one man in town who ought to know where they're headed next."

"You want to tell me, old man, or do I have to guess?" Rudy prompted him impatiently.

The cleaner blew his nose into the dust heap he was sweeping, and paused just long enough to give the required information.

"Jack Drummond. His office is in the mail building. Can't miss him. Best of luck."

Rudy spoke his thanks in a low voice, which might have meant that the deaf cleaner did not hear it at all. Jack Drummond turned out to be a portly fellow in his middle fifties. A businessman with an eye to a quick turn of profit. He was short in stature, with a glass eye, a wing collar and a derby hat, which he wore habitually, far back on his head.

From a rickety swivel chair, he asked: "Something I can do for you, stranger?"

Rudy nodded, smiled and offered him a small cigar. Drummond took up the offer, glanced at the wall-clock, as though about to time the interview and bullied a big match-stick into flame on his boot. When they were both smoking easily, Rudy mentioned his business.

"I was late hittin' town last night. Wanted to talk to a special act. A duo. Thought one of the pair could furnish me with a bit of information."

"Are you in show business yourself, may I ask?"

Rudy shook his head. "No, I'm up from Salt Creek, askin' questions on account of a tragedy that happened a short while ago. At first, I thought Clinton Church might be able to help me. But he didn't. So now I want to talk to Lolita an' Leopoldo. Lolita, in particular, I guess."

Drummond removed the cigar from

his mouth and regarded the glowing end of it rather closely. He also stared at some of the posters and sketches which graced the walls of his office.

"I don't want to pry too closely into this tragedy of yours, but Lolita, as he's billed, is tough to deal with, at times. Let's say his temper varies. A bad man to cross. His name's Ringo Spade. I don't know a lot about his partner, though. Took up with him two or three years ago. They're a strange couple."

Just when Rudy thought the agent was about to open up and feed him some worthwhile information, the unpredictable fellow dried up and acted like he was impatient. He put on a bold smile, and bustled about. "I'd take it as an act of kindness if you wouldn't tell Ringo who you've talked to. That is, in the event of you catchin' up with him. As I'm rather busy, I'll have to ask you to leave now."

Hiding his disappointment, Rudy shook hands and came out of the office.

The track of the Texas-California railroad was a few hundred yards north of the settlement. No one, apparently, required the train to stop regularly at Saguaro, so no attempt had been made to construct a proper platform. This lack of special facility, however, did not disappoint Rudy, because about fifty yards down the track approaches he had spotted a lightweight cart with a sagging, patched green canvas top.

Two men, one young and the other middle-aged, were running a pair of stocky chestnut horses into the shafts, prior to moving on. Rudy's pulse quickened. Both of them looked a whole lot different from Lolita and Leopoldo, and yet he had a feeling that his luck had changed. Here, unless he was mistaken, was none other than Ringo Spade and his mysterious young partner.

Leopoldo gave a different impression from when he was on stage. He was about five feet ten inches tall, not much over nine stones in weight and pale of complexion. His expression was hard-set for someone in his twenties. The blue eyes reflected very little in the way of emotion. He was like a man trained to poker, or one who had some sort of withdrawal symptoms.

By contrast, Lolita, or Ringo Spade, as he appeared to be called, now looked anything but effeminate. In his late thirties, he was a shade shorter in height than his partner. As to his weight, he was bulky, but muscular, and looked to weigh anything up to fourteen stones. His eyes were dark and deep-set under a bony forehead. His skin was sallow and his expression sullen.

"Good day to you, boys," Rudy called, as he came nearer.

Spade paused, his fingers busy with a strap. He glanced in the direction of his partner and then acknowledged the greeting with a curt nod. Rudy approached still closer and came to a stop, just a couple of yards from the restless chestnuts.

"Go mount up, Dick," Spade suggested, as the young man hovered behind him.

Dick hastily licked his dry red lips, and then complied, hurrying round the far side of the animals and springing adroitly up onto the box.

"You got a message for us, stranger?" Spade asked.

"Not a message. I did want a minute or two to speak with you, if you weren't too rushed. In fact, I thought you'd left town earlier."

"Make it a half-minute an' you've got a deal," Spade returned smoothly.

He hauled a tobacco-sack from the breast pocket of his straining blue shirt and busied his fingers with making a cigarette. Rudy offered a small cigar, but Spade declined rather casually.

"I hit town just in time to take in your act last night," Rudy began. "You were great. I wondered if I might see your — er — props, costumes an' that sort of thing."

"All props an' costumes are packed.

We're about to move on, as you can see. Besides, it's considered to bring bad luck, showin' a stranger a performer's gear. Hope you won't be disappointed too much." As an afterthought, Spade added. "Was there any particular item of gear you were specially interested in?"

Rudy grinned good-humouredly. He toyed with his cigar without lighting it. "Sure, I come from a town further south. Just a day or two ago, a fellow was killed in a hotel. Not far from the body was a woman's wig. All long blonde hair, you know. I wanted to ask you if you had any theories about wigs. I mean about why an elderly man might be carrying such a thing in his baggage."

The youthful character up on the box did not seem to have the slightest interest in Rudy, or in his questions, but Spade reacted far differently. Mounting up onto the box, he narrowed his eyes and slanted a sidelong glance in Rudy's direction.

"Now see here, *amigo*, I hope you didn't come a long distance just to ask me a fool question like that. Me, I use a wig now and again to entertain the public. Makes me look different, is all. It amuses western audiences. A man who is travellin' maybe bought a wig as a present for a pretty woman. Ain't you makin' a big issue out of a small item?"

Rudy nodded. "If you're lookin' for a murderer an' you don't have a whole lot to go on, you follow up any sort of a lead, however slight, Mr Spade. However, I hope I didn't delay you too long."

Ringo controlled his surprise at hearing his real name in use, and he fidgeted on the box beside his companion to mask his real feelings.

"What did you say your name was?"

"Rudy Girton, town marshal of Salt Creek City. I'll hope to take in your act again, some time. Adios!"

"Yer, yer, *adios*, Girton," Spade replied brusquely. "You're a long way from home. I hope you get back all right."

Clearly, Spade had no particular affection for peace officers. He cracked his whip, gripped the reins and turned the lungeing pair of horses across the track. Spaces between the ties had been built up with timbers, so that a wagon could pass over without fouling its wheels. The wagon bumped over, shaking the men on the box, but not putting any particular strain on the shaft horses.

Spade turned them sharply on the other side so that they were heading towards the west. His whole body was tensed up. He was frowning so deeply that his eyes were narrowed to slits. The young man beside him shifted uneasily.

"Ringo, I can't figure out why that peace officer should worry you so much. Why should he upset you? He only wanted to ask questions about people who wear wigs. That wasn't so off-puttin', was it?"

Spade turned his head away. He sniffed and spat into the dust beside the wagon. "Oh, I don't know. Peace officers an' their questions do things to me. Him comin' all the way from that town, Salt Creek, to ask me about folks wearin' wigs. Made me feel guilty. As if he had me lined up for a crime, or something. Maybe I'm over touchy, or something!"

"I think you're over touchy, Ringo," Dick remarked, after a short pause. "We were in that area, though, weren't we? Remember when I had that bout of fever, an' you left me in the wagon an' rode into town to get some pills? Wasn't that Salt Creek you went to?"

Ringo gave him a rather forced grin. "You're taxin' that hurt memory of yours, Dick, lad. Don't try too hard to recall everything in the past. Time will cure your ailment. No, it wasn't Salt Creek. It was South Creek. All right?"

Dick undid his blue bandanna and carefully mopped the perspiration from his brow. He seemed particularly conscious of the red mark across his forehead, put there by the band of his flat-crowned stiff-brimmed cream stetson.

"You know, I think you're right, Ringo. Me, I didn't think there *was* a place called South Creek. Not anywhere in these parts. Just goes to show, don't it? I don't reckon I ought to start tryin' to recollect what happened beyond the accident. Not yet."

Ringo nodded a few times. He was wrapped up in his own private thoughts quite exclusively for a time. The dust built up behind them. Up ahead, the terrain looked formidable. All arid soil, dust, rocks, boulders and heat shimmer. And the occasional, inevitable stand of cactus, and yellowing stunted grass.

Dick was ready to ask questions about their next stopping-place when Ringo checked the horse-team, coughed on the extra dust the manoeuvre caused, and slowly hauled the whole outfit in a tight half-circle to face the way they had come.

"It's all arid, my lad, up that way. Badlands, and not much more. Besides, I figure we ought to go see our buddies some time soon. And your sister, huh?" A smile flickered on and off young Dick's face. Clearly, he was composing words to ask questions about riding towards the badlands.

Ringo forestalled him. "Aw, I only went off that way because the peace officer back there had riled me. I don't like bein' asked questions by badge toters, see? An' I ain't alone. Thousands like me shun the likes of him on every possible occasion. So quit taxin' that tired brain of yours, an' relax."

Ringo chuckled. He flicked the reins. The two horses responded. Soon, the outfit was back where it had started westward on the north side of the rails. On they went, towards the east and, later, further north.

* * *

Quite by chance Rudy Girton encountered Jack Drummond, the agent, in a saloon. He bought him a large whiskey and chatted about this and that, finally mentioning that he had made contact with Spade and his partner before they left town.

Drummond blinked his glass eye. "That bein' so, now you will know all you needed to ask him. An' as you're unharmed, I guess he didn't turn nasty, huh?"

"Not exactly. He said I was wastin' my time, askin' fool questions about a wig. He hoped I'd get back all right, then he crossed the railroad track an' made off towards the west as fast as his team could go."

"I'm sure you meant the east, *amigo*, 'cause there's nothin' to westward except thirst an' badlands!"

Drummond was so surprised, he had a coughing fit to follow his laughter. When he recovered, Girton had gone.

Rudy checked out what Drummond had said about the badlands to westward, found it to be true, and himself left town on horseback about an hour later. He headed east, and then north-east, and soon he had settled down to a useful riding rhythm. He felt assured that Ringo Spade knew a whole lot more about what he needed to know than he had revealed.

Nevertheless, sleep was winning a battle to close his eyes a few hundred yards north of Two-mile Rock when a rifle bullet knocked sparks from the eroded stones between the dun's forefeet.

Badly startled, the white-blazed animal threw up its forelegs, pivoted on its hindlegs and abruptly dumped its dozing rider on his back in the dust. His head struck a trail-side boulder. His senses left him at once.

The dun trotted uncertainly forward for two hundred yards. Its progress ceased when the reins snagged over a bush.

7

ISAAC LAMONT had lived long enough to prefer his own company. In three-score years he had spent a whole lot of time on the trails of the west, and being of a loquacious nature he often talked to himself. On an average he wore out a pipe every two or three months, which was to be expected because he had a pipe stem in his mouth at all times, except when he was eating or sleeping.

He was a lean, dried-out undersized fellow with a kite-shaped face quite like seamed leather. A neat tuft of white chin beard extended his face somewhat, and a tall stetson, pinched almost to a point over the crown, made him look a little like a pixie. He was tough. His gentle high-pitched voice had often led others to think him a pushover, but this he was not.

The peculiar singsong voice was the first thing Rudy Girton knew when he returned to consciousness.

"Hell an' tarnation, why does a fellow have to find the owner when he's just discovered a fine dun horse with years of stamina still in him? I find the horse, hung up like a gift on a Christmas tree, an' here is its owner, I surely shouldn't wonder!"

Lamont slowed his buckboard for the second time in fifteen minutes. He had the runaway dun tethered to the board at the rear. His Alsatian dog, a powerful brute with a wolfish expression, yelped, and jumped down to the trail to examine the fallen body.

Lamont spat out of the side of his mouth without removing his pipe. "Now, look, Romulus, mind how you deal with the fellow. If he's in a bad way you'll frighten him to death, an' if he recovers too quickly he might shoot you for a wolf!"

Most of this talk Rudy heard and understood, although for a time he was aware of a sick feeling in his head and a curious, detached impression that he was in a spot he had never visited before. His nose remarked on tobacco before the big Alsatian licked him. He blinked himself conscious as the creature whined near him, and by the time the veteran traveller had dismounted and crossed to his side he was able to cautiously raise his head on his crooked arm.

"Howdy, partner," he remarked. "My head ain't too good. Would you mind tellin' me exactly where we are?"

"On a dusty trail, a piece further north than the landmark known in this county as Two-Mile Rock. Are you able to take that in at all?"

Rudy nodded, regretted it and lowered his head slowly. Clicking his tongue, Lamont went back to his conveyance and came back with a canteen of tepid water. The fallen man slaked his thirst greedily and made an effort to clear his thoughts.

"I'm glad to see you found my

cayuse, mister. I don't figure I'll stay in business long if I lose him. Say, I'm in your debt. You wouldn't want to offer me a ride back into town on that buckboard, would you?"

"My old Ma used to say to me, 'Isaac, my boy, you're a real good fellow. One day, you could turn out to be a good Samaritan, like the fellow in the Bible parable, you know'."

Lamont chuckled, blowing some burning tobacco out of his pipe.

"I reckon a couple of fingers of whiskey would do you good, young man. If you can stagger to your feet an' get to the 'board I'll guarantee you a strong drink as a reward."

Rudy chuckled, in spite of his discomfort. He managed to raise himself and reach the buckboard before his impaired balance made him stagger. The whiskey did him good, and had him reflecting that he had been able to cut down on strong liquor since he set out from his base on this unpredictable mission.

Lamont talked of this and that, revealed that he was a newspaper proprietor in Saguaro, and filled in his passenger with an outline of his wanderings in the north-east part of the county in search of copy for his weekly paper.

By the time the old man began to tire, his pipe was low on fuel and Rudy had recovered a little.

"Mr Lamont, did you by any chance see anyone around, shortly before you located my horse?"

"Can't say I did, Rudy, on account of I was resting off the east side of the trail, an' sort of composin' copy for my next issue with my hat over my face."

Rudy deduced from that statement that his benefactor had been sleeping. He could not blame him for that. But Lamont gave the impression that his mind was usually on the alert, and the younger man probed with another question.

"Did you hear a gunshot of any sort?"

Lamont slowed up on the reloading of his pipe and blinked thoughtfully. He studied his questioner's face, guessing at the reason for the question.

"Are you sayin' that your present condition had to do with a hostile gunshot, *amigo*?"

"I was dozin' at the time, Isaac, an' somebody fired off a rifle at a distance. The bullet struck the trail right between the forelegs of that dun back there. I was thrown. Hit my head, an' didn't know any more."

"Any idea who did it?"

"Not anything I could prove, anyways. That's why I was so keen on askin' you. I made contact with a couple of fellows earlier in the day. Travellin' entertainers, they were. And I had the impression they didn't like me askin' questions. Only thing was, they left quite some time ago, an' didn't have any real reason to know I might be following them up."

After a pause, Isaac asked: "Do you have any special reason for askin' questions, Rudy?"

"Sure enough. When I'm at home, I'm the town marshal of Salt Creek City. The questions are about items left by a man who was stabbed to death in Salt Creek. A man named Haymes, who was searching for his family. Got separated from them maybe a couple of years ago. Following an attack on a locomotive by an outlaw gang, who blew apart a van an' set fire to a carriage, so I'm led to believe."

Lamont contrived to whistle through his teeth without removing his pipe-stem from his mouth. "It don't do to read too much into a hostile rifle-shot. Me, for instance, when I heard that gunshot, I only thought of someone blastin' off at a jackrabbit. Gettin' ready for an outdoor supper. Why don't we take it easy till we get back to town? Then I'll turn up my archives — the back numbers of my paper, an' see what I can find for you."

Rudy approved, with a beaming smile. Presently, he stopped trying to clear his thoughts and allowed the gentle motion of the buckboard to lull him into sleep.

* * *

Ninety minutes after their arrival in town the newspaper owner and the peace officer strolled up Second Street towards the building bearing the banner nameplate, the *Saguaro Sentinel*. Lamont had not yet started smoking after an evening meal. He was still working bits of beef out of his gapped teeth with a wooden tooth-pick. Rudy was content to smoke. His head had cleared. Having suffered this second crack on the head, he had denied himself both beer and whiskey. Coffee, however, appeared to have done him some good.

Inside the newspaper building there was a smell of printer's ink. It made the offices quite distinctive, and different. Rudy followed the owner to the private office which occupied a corner of the extensive ground floor, the inner walls being glassed about four feet from the ground.

The back numbers were kept in wide deep drawers with a lot of unnecessary dust, but Girton's cigar kept him from coughing and sneezing. Within ten minutes Lamont had out the yellowing copies of the *Sentinel* which related to the locomotive robbery along the line beyond Piute Junction, in the direction of the Texas border.

There were eye-witness accounts by the engineer and fireboy, and an interview with the conductor who had suffered the indignity of being hit over the head.

The room gradually filled up with pipe and cigar smoke, as the papers moved from hand to hand. Eventually, the two avid readers had finished, and the time had come to mull over what they had read and discuss some of the details.

"You still as interested, son?" Lamont asked, talking round his pipe.

"More than before, Isaac. Circumstances in my home town, Salt Creek, make it unlikely that I shall be welcome unless I find some evidence connected with the killing back there. I feel that locatin' this family might be the next best thing. One thing puzzled me. The accounts said the missin' folks were called van Groot. Whereas my corpse bore the name of Haymes. Wilbur Haymes. Now known to have been a property agent in Chicago."

Lamont nodded sagely. "I took an interest in that affair. I believe Wilbur Haymes was Juliana van Groot's second husband. She was younger. They travelled for pleasure. In this area, the south-west, the clean dry air was supposed to be good for Mrs van Groot's chest, on account of her havin' slight lung trouble.

"The girl an' the young fellow were fit enough, only they disappeared directly after that van was blown apart an' the passenger carriage caught fire. All that smoke . . . The Border gang had plenty of horses, an' it is believed the family was spirited away on horseback."

"I wonder why?" Rudy queried. "At first, as some sort of insurance, perhaps? Possibly to offer them up for ransom. Who knows?"

He explained once again about the fine blonde wig he had along with him, and asked his host what he thought of it.

"Somehow or another, Rudy, I believe I heard an account which suggested Mrs van Groot sustained burn injuries. Perhaps she lost that long hair of hers, an' Haymes wanted her to have a replacement as soon as he located her. Does that make sense to you?"

"It's quite an interestin' theory, Isaac, an' it might just be true. But tell me, these outlaws who pulled the train robbery. They've been active again, just recently. Whereabouts?"

"Further north a piece. In the next county. South Colorado. They moved in in force, pillaged and robbed a ranch an' went to ground again."

Rudy blinked and frowned and scowled at the nearest glass window, beyond the blooming light of the hanging lamp. His mind was busy with Haymes' family photograph again. He was thinking that if the mother had succumbed, where were the son and daughter? Listed as Martha and Dick, they ought to have survived. But how? Had Martha thrown in her lot as an outlaw's woman? Was it possible that Dick van Groot had become an outlaw?

Or was it possible that Dick's mind was in limbo, damaged possibly by the shock of the fire and what followed after? *Was it possible that Spade's young partner, Dick, was Dick van Groot?* Or was his — Rudy's mind off the beam? Carried away by an overactive imagination?

"How have they managed to keep clear of the posse for over two years, Isaac — ?"

"Why, by usin' their heads, I guess, Rudy. I figure they went off for a while to the north. Into Colorado state. For a time we didn't hear nothin' about them. Then again, they might have spent a good deal of time in the badlands, over to the north-west.

"They come an' go, do Link Border, Deac Schmidt an' the others. Restlessness is usually the undoing of an outfit like that. One day they'll take on too much, an' then the law will catch up with them. Maybe, you, yourself. Are you figurin' on tanglin' with them at all?"

Rudy's expression hardened. "If I have to tangle with them to get close to the van Groot family, then I surely will. Besides, my old buddy, Sam Callaway, is standin' in for me right now, back in Salt Creek, an' he has a hole in his leg, put there by one of the Border boys."

Lamont whistled, and this time he was not so successful on account of his pipe. A few burning embers sailed out of the bowl before he could recover.

"So that's where the federal marshal took off to. Said he was goin' to drop out for a while. Go see an' ol' comrade. Must've been you, he meant, I guess. So you do have a reason for goin' against the Border gang, apart from the one you mentioned, connected with the van Groots.

"You'll be movin' on to Arroyo, I guess. When are you thinkin' of leavin'?"

Rudy carefully rubbed out the butt of his cigar. In the short time he had come to know the old newspaper proprietor, he had formed an attachment for him.

"You'll be offerin' me a night's lodgin', Isaac, won't you? After breakfast will be soon enough, I suppose. Maybe you could send a telegraph for me to old Sam, in Salt Creek. A cunning message, telling him plenty between the lines. What do you think?"

Lamont chuckled and drew a pad towards him. Between them they concocted messages for over half an hour, whispering to one another like a couple of conspirators planning trouble.

A bout of yawning finally terminated their efforts and sent them in search of beds, within the building. Rudy retired, convinced that progress and peril together lay to the north.

8

THE town of Arroyo might at one time have been called Twin Rivers had not an early rancher settler considerably altered the settlement's prospects. In blasting some rock, so as to irrigate his lands more easily, the rancher in question had effectively cut off the water-supply to one stream and doubled the volume, more or less, in the other. Consequently, the township had one useful stream and a dried-out river bed which stayed that way, even in the fall.

Rudy Girton arrived in Arroyo during the third hour of the afternoon following his short sojourn with Isaac Lamont.

By this time his cravings for strong liquor had abated. He no longer felt like sampling the powerful Mexican drink known as tequila, and his thirst was the normal one occasioned by prolonged time working the dusty western trails.

He rode boldly into the new community, put up his horse in the nearest stable, and entered a bar directly after refreshing himself under a pump. Three pints of tepid beer away from dehydration, he made a slow walking-tour of the town, and decided it was an interesting place, without making a whole lot of progress in matters regarding the van Groots, or Wilbur Haymes.

After booking a room for the night he took a meal and sauntered out of doors again to use his eyes once more. He listened to a lot of conversations, and studied a few notices, but nowhere did he find evidence that Lolita and Leopoldo were in town, or anywhere near.

His evening quest left him feeling a little depressed, but at the same time he was developing some capacity for patience. The old boredom which had driven him to drink no longer assailed him, and his back did not bother him any more, as it had done when he first went back to protracted horse-riding.

He returned to the lodging-house, admired the landlady's crochet work, smoked before the log fire, and turned in early, convinced that one day soon his luck would have to change and something positive would have to happen in regard to his patient investigation.

At ten the following morning he encountered a veteran blacksmith who was on the point of leaving his forge for the nearest drinking-place. As he thought it worthwhile to ask a few questions of the blacksmith, Rudy followed him into the saloon, and arrived conveniently with him at the long bar.

"A long drink of beer, Patrick, isn't it?" the small dark barman murmured.

"Make that two, mister," Rudy suggested, "an' have one for yourself!"

Patrick, the smith, glanced round enquiringly, and returned Rudy's friendly grin with a slight nod which threw forward his big grey quiff of hair.

The barman fixed the two pints, but declined himself, reflecting that beer drunk too early after his breakfast coffee gave him indigestion. Side by side, the two men lifted their glasses. Rudy put on an act, as though noticing the leather apron and overalls for the first time.

"I suppose workin' in a smithy is thirsty work at any time?" he remarked, having sunk a third of the beer.

"It is, too," the smith replied, although he seemed anxious about gossiping during ordinary working-hours, away from his job.

"Do you know, I've been just about all over the town, tryin' to find traces of a couple of friends who came this way just ahead of me. I can't find them at all, but it occurs to me you might have had dealings with them through their shaft horses.

"Would you be recollectin' one or a pair of horses, chestnut in colour an' used to pulling a lightweight cart?"

The blacksmith's bushy brows came together. In keeping with most westerners he did not like to be questioned about others. He was suspicious. The effect of the question was to close his mind, make him withdraw into himself.

"Now see here, mister, I can see you're no stranger to the west, so you won't take offence if I decline to answer your questions, will you? All kinds of travellin' hombres go through Arroyo. I always find it best to deal with a man face to face, an' forget about him when he's moved on."

With that, the smith turned his back on his interrogator and gave all his attention to draining his big glass. Rudy merely shrugged his shoulders and regarded the other's sullen expression in the long mirror.

If anything could be read into the smith's talk, it meant that he did have some memory of chestnut shaft horses. Which was useful to know, but not very helpful.

The swarthy barman flitted along behind the bar, timing his arrival with the emptying of the smith's glass. He was about to compliment him on his ability to drink beer when he saw the smith's countenance change again. The batwings had opened, and standing just inside them was a figure which interested Rudy every bit as much as the blacksmith. There was no mistaking the pale, set features of the young man known as Dick, almost certainly Dick van Groot.

At once, the smith muttered fiercely. He was cursing to himself for being caught in the saloon when a client was waiting for him to finish a job. With an effort he cleared his glowering expression, turned away from the bar and the mirror and prepared to chat with the newcomer.

Rudy, whose senses were very much on the alert, suddenly saw an opportunity. He raised a hand, delayed the smith, and explained what he had in mind.

"Why, smith, that there is the young

fellow I so much wanted to talk with. Young Dick. Tell me, is it possible he's waitin' for something you have to do?"

With another big effort the smith fought down his displeasure over being restrained by Rudy, and asked him to repeat what he had said. The marshal showed a lot of restraint.

"I said if Dick is waiting for some work you haven't completed, I'd be glad to take him off your hands for a while. At least, that's what I really meant. Would it help?"

The smith groaned, and then beamed. "I'm sorry I was so short with you just now, but you can't be too careful these days. As a matter of fact he's come to collect one of those chestnuts you were on about. I was almost ready to fit the last shoe when something happened. There was a flaw in the metal. Very rare. It really threw me behind schedule. So let's go talk to him."

Rudy touched his hat to the barman

who had been watching all the goings-on with more than passing interest. He then went ahead of the smith and put on his most engaging smile for Dick van Groot.

"Hi, Dick, I'm Rudy Girton. I saw you just before you left Saguaro. Remember?"

Dick nodded. He toyed nervously with his blue bandanna and reseated his cream stetson, which had acquired a sweat-stain above the band since Rudy saw it last.

"Yer, I remember you, Rudy. Only I don't think my partner, Ringo, is very keen to have me talk with you."

The smith was still in the background, tactfully scratching his head as he waited for the reunion to be completed.

"Is Ringo in town, Dick?" Rudy pressed him.

"Well, no, he's out of town, doin' a bit of revolver practice by the wagon as a matter of fact."

"He doesn't need to know you an' I have met then. I want to talk to you for a short while, about Martha, an' the rest of your family, see?" Rudy turned to include the smith then, and raised his voice. "The smith here has about another half-hour's work on that there shaft horse of yours, so I'd be doin' him an' the two of us a favour if I kept you here to drink some beer. Will that be all right, smith?"

Dick still hovered about uncertainly, as if he was unsure of himself without the backing of the formidable Ringo, but the other two made allowances for him, and he capitulated.

Off went the smith, while Rudy steered Dick to a remote table and there lighted for him a small cigar. In a couple of minutes he had journeyed to the bar and returned with two more beers and two shot glasses of whiskey.

Dick was enjoying the cigar. He sucked furiously at it, until Rudy chided him in case he made himself sick. The pale young man started on the beer. As he sipped Rudy delved in his pockets and produced three newspaper cuttings and two photographs. One of the latter was the family group from Haymes' hotel room, and the other was of Wilbur Haymes alone, dressed in a formal business suit and looking like any other prosperous Chicago property agent.

"How come you know my name, Rudy? An' how come you've heard of my family? I was intrigued when I heard you say to Ringo that time about lookin' for a murderer."

Rudy gazed steadily into Dick's face. "It's my job, Dick. The murdered man was called Wilbur Haymes. That's him, there, on the photo. Do you recognize him?"

Dick appeared to turn paler from the area of his lips. He blinked several times, as though to push away from his mind the notion that his father — his stepfather, to be exact — had been murdered.

Rudy started to ask his last question again.

"Yes, sure, of course I recognize him.

But, well, why should an inoffensive little businessman like Wilbur Haymes get himself murdered? How can it be true?"

Rudy took a deep breath. He knew nothing about the effects of violent shock on the human mind, but Dick's memory was not in such a mess as he had anticipated.

"There was a prowler in his hotel room, Dick. Either he was killed by accident, so that he couldn't identify the thief, or the intruder knew him, an' for some reason didn't want him to succeed in findin' his family."

Dick blinked hard, studied Rudy's face, rejected the beer and reached for the whiskey. The drink steadied him.

"Wilbur was lookin' for Ma, an' Martha an' me?"

"I am absolutely certain of it. There were people in Salt Creek he had asked, before the tragedy happened. How come you an' Martha haven't sought out Wilbur before this happened?"

Dick drank some more whiskey. He

murmured: "Why did you leave out Ma?"

"Is she still around?" Rudy asked gently.

Dick shook his head. "She was in poor shape after the explosion aboard the train. She was never very strong. The flames got to her. She lost her hair, an' there were burns about her head and shoulders. No, she only lasted for a few days. I think it was best she didn't make it. The boys buried her real nice. Near the creek."

Rudy pushed the second whiskey-glass across the table.

"Dick, who are the boys you are talkin' about?"

The second glass of liquor went down more speedily. "The boys? Why, the boys, of course. Ringo's friends. The folks we've been stayin' with since the accident. Here, what am I doin' talkin' to you like this? You're plyin' me with spirits so I'll talk.

"Ringo warned me about this!" Dick's voice rose. Rudy wondered if his control was going to snap. One or two heads came round in the direction of their table, but the marshal held on, merely nodding understandingly, and patted Dick on the shoulder.

"What about Martha?" Rudy cut in firmly.

Dick faltered in his tirade. Rudy's unfaltering gaze helped to restore him. The restless movement of the blue eyes, which were no longer vacant, showed the intensity of his emotion.

"What about my sister?"

"Is she fit? Is she well? Are the boys givin' her a good time, or not?"

"The boys? Oh, they treat her with respect on account of Vegas Jack. The boys take notice of Vegas. Only, well, sometimes she looks tired, bored. She looks as if she wants to move on. Only Jack would be lonely then. An' the boys wouldn't want her to leave. Why are you askin' me all these questions?"

"Because I believe your partner, Ringo Spade, slipped into Salt Creek and stabbed Wilbur Haymes to death."

Conflicting emotions pulled Dick's features this way and that. It was over a minute before he could re-establish control of himself.

"But that doesn't make sense! Ringo has been good to me since the accident. My mind was bad. My memory didn't work properly for a while. He taught me things, how to perform on the stage an' such. Why should he want to murder my stepfather?"

"Has it ever occurred to you that Ringo an' the boys might have a special reason for keepin' tabs on you an' your sister?"

Dick groaned. He mopped his brow, stared round the saloon like a man in anguish, and gulped some of his beer.

"I sure wish we'd gone straight on to Blockhouse Valley. I really do! What was that special reason you were on about?"

"Your stepfather was a rich man. He had extensive property interests in

Chicago. So, when he died, someone would have to inherit. Now that your mother has passed on, that leaves you an' your sister, Martha.

"They could play you off, one against the other. If Ringo kept on the right side of you they could put you back into circulation an' put pressure on you to make over most of Haymes' holdings to them! Gettin' their hands on hundreds of thousands of dollars without havin' to raid a bank or blast a train might appeal to men who have been on the wrong side of the law for a long time. Especially if they feel like retiring."

Dick whistled. His mind ranged back and forth over Rudy's studied revelations. Every now and then his keen blue eyes returned to Girton's face. Eventually, he seemed to have digested all that had been said.

"I ain't never said Ringo an' me were runnin' with outlaws. An' after what you've said, I can't see myself pullin' away from Ringo an' the others with my sister back there up the draw." He held back on explaining where the draw actually was. "So, if you want to get us out, it would be up to you. Me, I haven't any confidence in the future. I don't rightly know who to trust any more. Right now, that horse must be ready. I don't want to know what you're plannin' because Ringo has the power to make me tell him almost anything. I'll go now. I've listened to you. What you told me makes me think life was easier when my memory wasn't workin'. *Adios*, Rudy. An' thanks for the drink."

He stood up, opened his mouth to say more, and then appeared to lose track of his thoughts. Rudy also rose to his feet.

"Speak privately to your sister, if you get the chance," he advised.

They shook hands. So as not to panic Dick, Rudy resumed his seat. He thought he had enough information in his head now to make some valuable headway, but for the life in him he could not think of an easy way to bring in Haymes' killer, or to rescue two young people from a whole gang of seasoned outlaws.

9

RUDY purposely stayed away from any place where Ringo Spade might be located. He strolled around the town, partook of a modest lunch in an eating-house run by two Italians, and then gravitated towards the glass-fronted two-entrance shop of Curly Smith, the town barber.

In the heat of the afternoon men often went to Curly's to have a shave or their hair trimmed, because it was good to sink back in his comfortable chairs and relax while he did his work.

Rudy had another motive in seeking out the barber's shop. It was one of the few places in a Western town where a man could gossip and not be thought of as an interfering busybody, or a spy of some sort.

Curly could either tell the tale, or he would whistle. On this occasion he had only one client ahead of Rudy, and he was in the higher of the two padded chairs with an off-white cloth draped round his neck and shoulders."

Rudy moved in, slowed down, found an unyielding bench against a rear wall and lowered his body into it, minus his hat.

"Good day to you, young fellow," Curly greeted him brightly.

The barber had a cut-throat razor poised over the client's head on one hand, and the other hand was pinching the nose. Soap covered the lower part of the customer's face, but clearly he was in for a shave and the removal of his moustache.

Rudy returned the greeting, stared at the man in the chair by way of the wall mirror, and wondered if their paths had ever crossed before. Discarded on the bench was a battered brown derby hat which had collected dust of every hue and description since it reached its present owner.

Rudy yawned. He picked up a

three-months-old copy of the *Frisco Times* and mechanically turned over a page. Curly had resumed his whistling, and the customer had relaxed in the chair. The brief tension in the client had nothing to do with Curly and the razor. He was the sort of fellow whose way of life makes it necessary to take a quick look at his fellow-men before they get too close.

Curly scraped methodically. His razor was sharp. He was adept with it. His work was easier to look at than the paper. Soon, Rudy discarded the latter and wondered if he could drum up a bit of information from the other two.

"It's a hot afternoon, an' I don't suppose you feel like talkin', but I was wonderin' if you had any idea how many chins you've scraped in this town?"

Curly was over forty-five years of age. He had run to fat. His own fair hair had thinned and was now creamed across his imposingly broad skull. To make up for his lack of natural thatch, he had grown a magnificent moustache and waxed it so that it extended outwards after the military fashion well beyond his plump cheeks.

The barber chuckled. "I'm no good at figures, *amigo*. A lot. Hundreds. Maybe a thousand or two. In shavin' an' haircuttin' I've never grown rich, an' I've never been short of a dollar for essentials. So it's a job, an' a man needs a job to keep his head up these days. One thing is on my side. I shave a man, his hair grows again. If he stays in town, he comes back to see me, or he has to shave himself. Maybe I'm gettin' to be a luxury with some galoots. Eh?"

Curly chattered on for a minute or two. He had almost finished working on the other man when Rudy asked his big question.

"Say, did you ever shave the chin of a friend of mine? I'm lookin' for him right now. Name of Jack. Vegas Jack, men called him on account of earlier associations. I heard tell he'd settled in a valley somewhere close to Arroyo."

The eroded eyes of the customer sharpened up, and then went deliberately blank again. Rudy had seen enough to feel that the owner of the brown derby had useful information.

Curly started upon a dissertation of all the men named Jack whom he had known. He talked glibly, but nothing he said specially interested Rudy, or the short compact man who was having his shiny brown suit brushed down.

Curly finished grooming his client and respectfully stood back with the brush and white cloth in his hands. He awaited the payment. The client studied himself in the big mirror, clearly was more than just satisfied. He dipped into his waistcoat pocket and made a big play of fishing out a silver coin, one which looked like a dollar.

Curly received it from him and backed out of the way, fingering the dollar as if its smooth edges gave him some satisfaction. He glanced down at it, and his expression changed.

"Hey, now, hold on a minute, I don't object to a silver coin of the realm, but this here object looks like it came from some South American coffee republic. It ain't legal in these parts. So if you wouldn't mind."

A slight tension developed in the shop. Rudy was aware of it at once. The client drew himself up to his full height and started to go through his pockets. He had a neat, compact figure, but he was no bigger than the average jockey in size. Curly and Rudy both realized before he had finished his search that he had no more money.

Rudy acted upon impulse. "If it will save you goin' back to your hotel I'll pay the money for you," he offered.

The tension began to subside again. The South American coin was handed back. Rudy paid, and the little man began to chuckle.

"It sure is kind of you, *amigo*."

He looked as if he meant it, too. As Rudy went under the cover in the second chair the little man glanced at his formidable derby hat and decided to stay a little longer. He had noticed a magazine which he had not seen before.

Before starting on Rudy's chin and hair Curly opened both doors a little way to ensure a slight draught of air. There was a sound out on the sidewalk, but no one in the shop reacted to it. The man with the derby sank down into a corner with the magazine well up to his face. He started to hum a melody, while Curly, who was clipping away tufts of Rudy's crisp dark hair, started his whistling again.

Two bulky men in riding-clothes came in off the sidewalk and seated themselves without any fuss in two chairs at the opposite end of the establishment to the earlier client. Suddenly, the humming stopped, and the small fellow chuckled.

In a voice which was big for his body, he remarked: "I've been thinking about what you said earlier, *amigo*. About wantin' to contact Vegas Jack, an' all.

If the fee was right I believe I could tell you exactly where to find him. Or take you, if you wanted company, only that might come a little more expensive!"

Rudy leaned forward in the chair. Curly paused in his labours, while the two newcomers shifted ominously on the lightly-built upright chairs which held them. Suddenly, the small man became aware of them.

They were hard-eyed men, both toting heavy gunbelts. Four revolvers between them. Instead of discarding the gun-belts, as they had intended, they fondled their holsters and leaned sideways, keenly interested in the speaker.

The hollow cheeks of the small man seemed pale after his overdue shave, and the removal of his moustache, but now his features blanched still more. He realized that he had spoken recklessly in the presence of the two gun-slingers. He shook off his fearful inertia, leapt to his feet and grabbed his hat. He was across the floor and out of the other door before anyone could react.

He murmured. "I've just remembered. The horseshoe tossin' contest down the street. *Adios*."

Curly and Rudy exchanged glances in the mirror. The hair clipping was resumed. The barber could see what manner of men had caused the sudden panic. He was equal to the occasion.

"I don't recollect you askin' any questions about no Vegas Jack, friend. Did I miss something a while back?"

Rudy puckered his face and frowned at the mirror. "I was singin' a song when I came in, something about Vegas. Didn't ask no questions as I can remember, barber. A little on the strange side, that jasper was, if you ask me."

He shrugged, and settled down again, marvelling how easily the lie had been spoken. In the meantime the two hostile characters had a whispered exchange of views and tacitly decided that they would come back later. As soon as they had removed themselves, Curly and his surprised customer breathed more easily.

"Our little mate certainly stirred up something," Rudy commented, uneasily. "Thanks for easin' me out of an unusual situation."

Curly stepped to the door and put his comb through his thinning hair. "I don't like to think a client of mine hits trouble through anything that happened in my shop. They've gone after him, you know. Seems you touched a raw nerve of some sort when you mentioned that character Vegas Jack."

Rudy nodded, and resumed his place in the chair. "I don't know if you'll believe me now, but I've never seen the fellow. I do hope to locate him, though, on account of a family I'm seekin'. Folks who dropped out of sight a couple of years ago."

Curly got back to his work, and Rudy became silent. In spite of his surprise, the small character looked as if he knew how to keep out of trouble. Ten minutes later the shaving was over. Rudy paid up and thanked the barber quite warmly, and intimated that he still intended to try to contact the little man, and to try to keep him out of trouble.

The horseshoe tossing contest was poorly supported in the afternoon because of the oppressive heat. Somewhere between thirty and forty townsfolk, mostly males, were at the open square where the bales had been put down as boundary markers for the contest.

A few dollars changed hands as men gambled on the results. Rudy was only interested in the whereabouts of his elusive acquaintance. The two watchful gunslingers were seated in the comparative shade of the nearest sidewalk, watching the proceedings with their hats pushed forward over their eyes.

Of the little man, there was no sign. Rudy was disappointed in himself, and at the same time relieved. Just as he was about to leave the area, having watched for ten minutes, he noticed a tall slim swarthy character with the build of a Mexican. This fellow had on a derby hat. *The* derby hat. And the shiny brown jacket of the missing man hung tightly about his shoulders like a bolero.

So that was it. 'Shorty' had swopped his give-away hat and jacket for the Mexican's gear. How long would it be before the gunmen noticed the incongruous appearance of the cheroot-smoking Mexican?

Keeping his eyes averted, Rudy moved away again. He hoped he had not been seen. One hour later he found the small man, who answered to Hank Derby, drinking lukewarm beer in a Mexican *cantina*. Obviously, he had found some more money, or the proprietor had accepted the South American coin.

Rudy moved to the bar, ordered two drinks, and took them along to the secluded alcove, where Derby fought down his sudden panic and accepted the drink gratefully.

"Hey, *amigo*, you haven't brought those two gunnies in my direction have you?"

Rudy sat down beside him. The new arrival grounded the drinks, mopped his brow and shook his head. In spite of himself, Rudy was forced to grin. The startled, hollow-cheeked face under the weathered sombrero looked anything but natural.

"Forgive me, *amigo*. I didn't chase after you on account of the haircut money, either. The way those boys reacted back there in the shop made me think there was a whole lot more to meetin' Vegas Jack than I first thought. I don't really know him, you understand. But I have to talk with him."

Derby covered Rudy's hands with his own. "Land's sakes, don't keep usin' that fellow's name, friend. You never know who might be listenin'."

The small man tilted back his sombrero to give him a clearer view of the rest of the *cantina*. He was just relaxing when something new caught his eye. His hairless face blanched. He lowered his head, noisily drank the new drink, and moved sideways out of his chair, catfooting towards the open upper part of the adobe wall at the back of the alcove.

"Hell an' tarnation, *amigo*, keep that stetson of yours well down. It's the only one in the building right now, an' those two gun-hawks have just arrived. Either they're lookin' for you or me, or both! If you follow me, make tracks for yourself. Do me that much of a favour."

So saying, Hank Derby put his hands on the wall opening, vaulted so that he could roll on it, and disappeared from view.

Acting upon Derby's sage advice, Rudy bent down as though to examine his boot. From a low angle he glanced across the establishment and quickly confirmed that the two gunmen had indeed arrived and, furthermore, they were still clearly looking for somebody.

As he had no weapon with him Rudy followed Derby's example, cautiously evacuating by the same route. Down in the dust of the alley, he straightened up and made for the thoroughfare. Just as he turned into it the head of the taller gunman appeared at the wall opening. He had been observed. By doubling across a couple of vacant lots he kept them off his back.

Being pursued within the boundaries of a town was a relatively new experience for him. He felt the adrenalin running through his body. He went to earth, and when next he appeared in the open he had his right-hand .45 Colt and gun-belt with him. He figured it would be too late to protest to the local peace officers if he ended up with a bullet in his back through not taking precautions.

Arroyo was in the grip of twilight when the latter stages of the horseshoe contest were reached. Many lamps had been strung on poles to offset the encroaching darkness. In the knockout competition, Hank Derby had reached the last four. He had taken on a few fingers of strong liquor and temporarily forgotten the menace of the two men who sought him. The brown derby was back on his head and his speech was very slightly slurred.

Rudy elbowed his way to the front of the crowd in time to see Hank go off down the far end, having tossed his shoes in the wake of his semi-final rival. A roar of interest came from the throats of the swaying crowd. A shopkeeper, acting as judge, cleared his throat and gave a decision. It went against Hank, who looked as if he was going to take it in a sporting fashion. But as he stepped forward to shake hands his startled eyes noticed the two gunmen, once again, and his confidence at once ebbed. His hand shook. He looked around, knowing he was hemmed in by the excited crowd.

Derby's expression changed. He picked up a horseshoe, gripped it tightly, and took a wild swing at the judge's head with it. The crowd gasped in surprise. There were raucous cries of protest. Derby feigned a reaction, pretending he was angry at the outcome of the contest. He broke free from the restraining hands of two officials and managed to knock off the judge's tall hat. Before he could be secured again he had struck one of the constables a glancing blow on the head. To prevent a riot the deputy marshal and two others grabbed him firmly and demanded for a path to be made through the onlookers. This was done with some show of reluctance, as wagers had been placed on Derby, and quite a few men had hoped to win money on him. Having backed a loser, they were now reminded that he was also a bad loser.

All this Rudy Girton took in. He was possibly the only onlooker who knew why Derby had acted the way he did. From a distance the marshal of Salt Creek witnessed his elusive ally being dragged into the jail. In spite of himself, Rudy could not help smiling at Derby's inventiveness. To be in the lock-up was to be safe from prowling gunmen, at least temporarily.

An anaemic moon was faintly sorting out the shadows of the sleeping town when Girton tossed a small stone through the open grille of the peace office cell and heard it fall on something soft. Derby stirred, made noises like a mangy dog, and finally sat up.

"Hey, who is that?" he hissed, in a controlled whisper. "Ain't I safe, even in here?"

"Your old buddy, Rudy Girton, *amigo*. I thought it was real slick of you to get yourself run in to avoid the gun-hawks."

There was a short pause. No other human reacted in the building.

"Okay, Rudy, this is Hank. Hank

Derby. You don't give up easy, do you? You can throw my bail money through the grille. I'll tell you what you want to know. Vegas Jack is a blind man. Some folks think he has, well, special powers. Can read the future, if you know what I mean. He lives about four miles north-east of this burg. In a remote valley called Blockhouse Creek. Creek or Valley, that is.

"These days, Jack's place has become a hideout or safe house for a vicious bunch of outlaws. Some say it's the Border boys. No doubt that pair from the barber's are members of the gang. Doin' a listenin' job in town. Actin' as spies. I ain't goin' near Blockhouse. If you go be careful. My advice is 'don't'."

After a pause, Rudy lobbed a pebble with five dollars wrapped round it through the opening. Using the string attachment, he lowered it down on the inside. Hank acknowledged its receipt, and they whispered their farewells.

Rudy then withdrew before they were discovered. As he crept away, in the shadows, he reflected how ludicrous it was for a *bona fide* peace officer to be acting as he had done.

10

THE geography of the south-western states was and still is a network of surprises. Rudy Girton reflected upon this as he rode north from Arroyo an hour after dawn. He had taken precautions that he did not bring the two prowling gun-hawks with him, and then eaten his eggs and bacon in a borrowed skillet on a private fire.

Ever since he left Salt Creek (and it now seemed months ago) he had been working his way further and further north. Now, he was north of the fairly modern railroad which spanned Piute County from east to west, and far enough north to be approaching the region of doubtful terrain south of the mighty Canadian river and the southern borders of Colorado state.

The dust flipped up by the dun's

shoes was no different from a whole lot of trail-dust in that part of the world, and yet the going felt different. He knew he was riding into a critical phase of his life which was likely to change him or eliminate him. A time when he solved, or at least knew, all the facts about the late Wilbur Haymes and his elusive family.

Perhaps this trip into Blockhouse Valley had always been part of his destiny. Its name suggested that it had once played an important part in the Civil War of the 1860s. A blockhouse, he knew, usually signified a small temporary fort. How big this one was, or whether it was still standing, he was due to find out.

The blood pulsed through his veins, but not at any critical speed. Between two and three miles to the north his trigger-finger started to twitch a little, and he found himself hauling out his Winchester and checking over its vital moving parts. Other times, he might have taken time off from the trail as the sun mounted its offensive from the east, but on this occasion it was not to be.

Quite without warning he found himself at a fork in the trail. There was a stunted oak beside the track with a wooden notice nailed to it. Many years earlier a patient western gent had burned the information on it with a hot poker or iron. To the north was La Linea — the Line — and more distantly the state of Colorado. Branching off to the north-east was Blockhouse, and a down-pointing, crudely-drawn thumb suggested that it was not a good place to visit.

Somewhere up that fork was the outlaw hideout. How close, it was not easy to tell. Consequently, Rudy side-stepped any gun-shooting practice, which would have announced his presence to any dozing lookouts, and merely turned into the lesser track. He paused long enough to take a drink from his canteen, and then on.

Just over a mile up the lesser track,

when he was studying the undulating ground, the second sign came into view. This time it was on the west side, and suggested that it was a good thing to go that way and head for La Linea. A fair enough warning, he concluded, but not one which he intended to take. Vigilance, after this.

On again: noting the fine upstanding stands of timber, mostly pine or oak, and the frequent upthrusts of grey stone, often reaching a greater height than the foliage. The grass was sparse, but green. Soon, he was riding through a thin stand of mixed trees which broke up the sun and mottled the stony ground ahead of him. The gradient changed so that the going became slightly easier for the toiling dun. It snorted a couple of times and improved its stride. Rudy wondered at that. He wondered how the quadruped would make out in the eventual clash, which he believed was inevitable. Through the trees ahead he anticipated his first glimpse into the draw which held the blockhouse. That would be the time to expect trouble . . .

A brief bright light wide on the right heralded the rifle-bullet which whipped off his stetson and flung it upside down ten yards away at the foot of a pine. *Before the end of the trees . . .*

Now! In a flash he had fought down the immediate reaction, to dive out of the saddle and take the Winchester with him. He raised his hands, and so lived. Sitting quite motionless, and checking the dun with his knees, he waited.

The man in the buckskin outfit came through the trees from some sixty yards away without intimating that he was in a hurry. His rifle was held in a position so that he could go over to the offensive again without delay. The half-breed who came from the opposite direction ghosted from tree to tree and eased up within five yards. He had only thirty yards to cover at the most. The keepers of Blockhouse Valley were skilled professionals.

"You want I should dismount, friends?" Rudy asked calmly. "Didn't know I was trespassin'."

The man in buckskins wore a straw hat shaped like a stetson. He had the sort of restless grey eyes possessed by a man used to living away from humans. In fact, he had lived as a trapper for many years: before he acquired the limp which changed his way of life.

His Apache partner was also around the forty-year mark, with the usual high cheekbones, and a wide, lined forehead. His dark, greasy hair was trimmed around his head at ear level. He wore a dark shirt, denims and a black pillbox hat with a stiff brim. He held his long-barrelled rifle as if it were a twig. A throwing-knife was partially concealed in the other hand.

"Your business? Do you have business in these parts?"

The buckskin character sounded almost polite, having just blasted a man's hat off his head. Rudy kept a straight face, thinking hard. Perhaps he ought to confess to something like the truth, for a start.

He murmured: "Sure. I came to see the blind person who lives down the valley. On account of a certain Wilbur Haymes, who has lost his daughter these two years an' wants to find her. Does that sound reasonable to you?"

The guards read each other's unspoken thoughts. The Indian passed back the initiative to the white man.

"What is the name of this blind person you spoke of?"

"As I heard it, he is called Vegas Jack. Will he see me, do you think?"

The talking guard sniffed. "It is possible," he conceded.

"How will I know the place?" Rudy asked.

"Follow the winding track to the lower ground. You will see the blockhouse nestling in the trees this side of the water. Usually, a lamp burns indoors an' there are pigeons around the building. A warning. There is no hidin'-place for a stranger in this neck of the woods. Take no liberties. Always you will be under observation."

Rudy nodded, and twitched his fingers. 'Buckskin' nodded, and the intruder lowered his arms. A movement on his other side startled him afresh, but he was not in any danger. The Apache had moved further away, hooked up the fallen stetson with the barrel of his gun, and was offering it: still dangling from the muzzle.

"Many thanks, *amigo*," Rudy remarked coolly.

He received it, took a long studied look through the twin holes above the band, and replaced it on his head. He was aware of the slight smell of burning material. It made his sensitive nostrils twitch. Nodding to first one guard, and then the other, he walked the twitching dun forward and schooled himself not to look back.

Five minutes later he had topped a slight rise and was descending the concave slope of short lush grass which led down to the lower reaches of the valley, where the creek might be expected. Stands of timber to right and left broke up the horizon and quivered slightly in the painted sky.

It all looked peaceful at first. A colony of high-nesting black birds circled and quarrelled in one of the highest tree clumps. Here and there a jackrabbit spurted across the open ground, or sat quite still, freezing into the landscape between the mole-hills and the warrened area.

The pigeons cooed and flew about, fanning their tails and taking their exercise. The blockhouse itself was a big square log cabin with a paddock at the rear and a small central look-out post upstanding on the roof. It was unmanned, judging by the wide open slits in the sides, and Rudy surmised that manning of the house itself was unnecessary on account of the widespread guards, working to a system around the periphery of the valley. His questing eyes studied the high ground on either side, and in the far distance.

There were frequent outcrops of rock and clusters of grey boulders which were so regular that they looked as if they had been planted in some sort of order.

They appeared almost like the battlements of some medieval fort, and raised a question as to how many guards would be needed at any one time to preserve the sanctity of the valley and keep out intruders.

A few pigs sported in thin scrub in the low land to the left, while a few sheep with lambs grazed a slope on the other side. There were cows in groups, further off.

The dun was still nearly a hundred yards away when the owner of the blockhouse casually appeared in a window opening, facing the direction of the rider's approach. He was well over six feet in height with a fine head of long white hair, and a grizzled beard and moustache. His facial skin was pockmarked and burned almost to the colour of mahogany. His eyes had a silvery, unsighted quality, which tended to rivet the attention of newcomers. He had lost his sight some years earlier when — as a river-boat gambler — a faulty Derringer pistol had exploded too near to his face.

He leaned forward, his ears already telling him much about the approach of the stranger. The big brown hands disappeared off the sill and immediately reappeared holding a megaphone, sometimes referred to as a bull horn. Vegas Jack put it to his lips.

"Ahoy, there, stranger! Keep on comin', but I'd be obliged for a few details about you before you get here! Strangers ain't often admitted. Me, I'm old. I like time to adjust to new things, new people!"

A rich, deep voice which would have been a great attribute to an actor rolled and rippled round the valley, giving Girton the impression that he was hemmed in on all sides. A dark-haired Indian girl dressed in a

165

thin hide tunic came from round the back, tucking away wisps of jet black hair which had escaped her hair band, poking them back into place. She had the darkest brown eyes Girton had ever seen. The ghost of a smile flickered around the corners of her wide mouth as she catfooted over to him, treading lightly in small moccasins to accept his horse.

The dun made no fuss as its master dismounted and the strange girl accepted the reins.

Rudy said: "My name is Girton. Rudy Girton. I come from Salt Creek. On account of a certain happening in my town, I'm lookin' for a girl, Martha van Groot, who went amissin' about two years ago."

The Indian girl hesitated on her way to the stable with the dun. She jangled the harness as she waited at the beginning of a thirty-yard pole fence which led to the shed full of stalls.

"Just give him a rub down and a light feed, Delfina," the blind man called, and then addressing himself to Rudy, he asked: "Why do you search for the girl?"

"Because her father has searched continuously to find her since she disappeared, an' now he is dead. You could say I am actin' for her deceased kin."

The megaphone was withdrawn, and one of the huge hands indicated for the visitor to enter. He took off his hat, knocked on the door and went in. The big living-room took up a good quarter of the house. It had padded chairs, a sofa, a hardwood table, and various smaller pieces of furniture.

Near an outer wall was a wide fireplace built on a large stone flag, which still showed the ashes of the last log fire. A pair of antlers decorated the wall above the fire, and colour-wash pictures were tacked against other wall surfaces.

There was a homely smell compounded of wood smoke, food, tobacco and old timber. Vegas Jack lowered himself into a large rocking-chair and snapped his fingers for Rudy to step closer. They shook hands, and Jack used his sensitive fingers to explore his visitor's arm and shoulder before they parted, and the latter occupied an upright chair.

"Keep thinkin' about the overhead beams, Mr Girton," Jack advised. "Me, I've grown used to knockin' my head, an' I crouch automatically when I stand up. So you want to contact Martha, eh? I don't rightly suppose I have the right to stop you talkin' to her. I could tell you she had a shockin' experience two years an' more ago. Connected with an explosion on the railroad. Since then she's lived in this valley, an' its calm seems to suit her. I surely hope what you have to say won't disturb her too much. I wouldn't like to think of her leavin'."

Rudy busied himself lighting Jack's pipe for him, and then put a match to one of his small cigars. "She's grown up enough to hear of her father's death," Rudy remarked. "Until this time, she doesn't know me, an' I don't intend to make her life more complicated than what it is. That's to say, I won't go against her best interests. Well now, if you'll be kind enough to call her I'd be obliged. I've been kind of impatient since a fellow shot my hat off back there."

Vegas stopped the rocker. The solemnity of his expression was suddenly transformed by a huge laugh which spread his mouth between beard and moustache. Rudy did not attempt to out-laugh the shack owner. Eventually, Jack calmed down. The rocker started up again.

"Blockhouse Valley sure has the finest bunch of guards in the west, Mr Girton. As you know to your cost. Would you care for some coffee?"

"I'd like to see Miss van Groot first," Rudy prompted him.

"In that case, you best be on your way, *amigo*. Keep right on down the valley. Soon, you'll locate the creek.

There is a useful island in the middle of it with a small huntin'-shack on it. That's Martha's private place. Around this time you could find her fishin'. When you get within earshot let her know who you are, 'cause she's kind of sensitive same as I am. You got that?"

Rudy rose to his feet. "I surely have, Jack. May I ask you a straight question before I go?"

Jack approved, and Rudy went on. "Is Martha free to come an' go from this territory any time she pleases?"

Jack rose slowly to his feet, his hand protectively above his head.

"*I* wouldn't stop her, Mr Girton, but there are other considerations . . . "

11

VEGAS talked obliquely about possible problems for anyone wanting to leave Blockhouse Creek, but he did not name the outlaw gang, nor did he suggest that a group of law-breakers had assumed control of his domain. He seemed cordial enough when he stepped into the open and called his farewell to the unexpected guest.

Delfina, the Indian maid, reappeared with the dun, as if by magic. The animal had been lightly groomed and fed, and looked fresh enough to start out on a protracted ride for the second time that day.

Between twelve and twenty pigeons circled the lookout platform on the roof and seemed to be saluting the rider as he moved off again. This time, he glanced back and waved to the girl, noting as he did so how the birds settled easily on the sill of the house, and how one of them flew down and perched on Delfina's wrist. He wondered then if it was possible to send messages by the birds, and where a man like Vegas Jack had acquired an Indian girl as a house-servant. Rudy thought the girl had a bright, intelligent face, and yet he did not recollect hearing her speak.

The terrain, and the imminent chance of meeting with Martha, brought his attention from the blockhouse area to what lay ahead. The path meandered for a while and suddenly dipped down to where he could see the spread of the creek. It looked shallow in some places, and yet he knew that the rays of the sun could give an entirely false impression of depths when the bright light was overhead.

Soon, he was skirting the waters. Although he was impatient, he paused long enough for his mount to slake its thirst at the water's edge, and — as he waited — he slopped water over his face and examined his chin to see how much stubble had appeared since he left Curly's barber shop in the last town. Fortunately, his facial hair did not grow very quickly, otherwise with his hair colouring he would have had an almost permanent blue chin.

A tiny mirror reflected the sun on a hogsback ridge to his right. He knew it was a mirror because whoever was holding it moved it adroitly, flashing a message in morse code to someone else in another key spot.

He kept his eyes on the alert, and then lost interest. It was only when he picked out the island from the line of the far bank of the creek that he had an inkling where the message had been received. The key point on the islet was highly placed among the masking trees. The message was not repeated. Horse and rider moved closer to the island, the quadruped enjoying the cool water around its feet while the man was full of anticipation for the next development.

A fantailed pigeon came down the valley from the blockhouse. He watched it adjust its flight until it turned into the tall trees and settled somewhere. It was almost as if a messenger had gone ahead of him. Five minutes later, a sturdy sapling flashed into the upright position just ahead of the dun, which was so startled that it almost jettisoned Rudy into the water.

He hung on as it pivoted on its hind legs and finally settled down again. Somehow or another a rope had been fixed to the sapling so that its upper half had been drawn down to water-level. The rope had been released on the other side of the creek: on the island, in fact. There were still signs of the rope writhing in the shallows.

"Ho, there!" Rudy called. "This is Rudy Girton attempting to make contact with Miss Martha van Groot, to talk on family business. Groot an' Haymes business, that is. Is it all right to cross over?"

After a brief pause a woman's voice

answered. "It's all right, stranger! This is Martha van Groot talkin'. Advance about twelve paces, then put your horse into the water. It's fordable there! I'll wait for you."

Not wanting to risk a ducking at the outset, Rudy carried out the instructions with great care. However, he was not at risk. The patch over which the dun walked was stony at bottom, but not sufficiently to be a serious difficulty.

Further to the right of the spot where he emerged at the other side were two fishing-lines, mounted on forked sticks. For a moment he saw no signs of his hostess. Further into the trees the hunting-lodge showed. He felt certain she was close, but he could not see her.

Having dismounted, he prowled the neat little shack, came out again and noticed the foot-holes chipped out of the timbers at one corner.

"You up there Martha?"

"Sure, I'm up here," the prompt

reply assured him.

She was not on the roof, but many feet higher on an oak tree, a branch of which hung closely over the shack roof. Martha came down in leisurely fashion with a battered spyglass hanging from her neck by a leather thong. He stood closer as she came down the side of the shack, but his assistance was superfluous. He could see that she was slim, and shapely, in spite of the leg-masking denims and the shapeless tunic. Her fair hair was of a very fine quality, arranged in plaits, one over each ear. A neat flat-crowned dun hat sat squarely upon her head. Her eyes were grey, and wide under a broad forehead. The nose, tip-tilted over full Cupid's bow lips. A black square of cloth, knotted like a bandanna, accentuated her long slim neck.

She wore a sheath-knife at her belt.

Rudy said: "Howdy, do you spend a lot of time lookin' through the glass?"

Martha chuckled. "Some women spend a lot of time looking *in* the glass, but not me. I asked for a glass to study nature, but it's good to note other things as well. Such as unexpected visitors. Men who come and go. You're not the last visitor today."

Rather belatedly Martha poked out her hand. Rudy shook it, and doffed his hat. They went indoors, and Martha at once grounded her coffee-pot on the top plate of a stove. Soon, it began to bubble.

The floor was of beaten earth, with a couple of mats to offset the hardness. A low-framed Indian-style bed occupied about a quarter of the interior. The only refinement lay in a loft, approached by a wooden ladder.

"What line of business are you in, Rudy?" the girl asked, taking off her hat.

She indicated the one upright chair, which only balanced when one of its legs dug well into the earth. Rudy took it. She sank down on the end of the bed, her legs in the cross-legged position.

"I'm a peace officer. Town marshal of Salt Creek City, well to the south, if you don't know it. Investigating a murder."

Martha gasped in surprise, and rose to her feet again. She bit her lip, frowned, and decided to pour out the coffee into the two mugs.

"Who — whose murder was it?"

This time Rudy moved to his feet and approached her. Something in his manner made her hand tremble. He added his own hand to the handle and together they poured. He made her sit down again, and handed her one of the mugs.

"You may resent me as much as every other person in these parts, Martha. I don't bring good news. The man who died was your stepfather, Wilbur Haymes. An intruder got to him. Wilbur was lookin' for you an' Dick an' your mother. So I followed up his enquiries. In case you could lead me to the killer."

As they sipped their coffee, he

outlined his motives, and what he had accomplished this far.

"When you talked to Jack, did he give you the impression you'd be allowed to leave, when you were ready, Rudy?"

The dark-haired young man shrugged. "We didn't discuss the matter, Martha. One thing I'd like to know from you, though. If you could, would you leave this valley an' seek to resume life as it was before that tragedy on the railroad?"

At this point tears escaped from the corners of Martha's grey eyes. She dabbed at them with the black bandanna. Rudy rose to his feet and tactfully moved over to the window, staring through it. He intimated that he was going to slip out for a minute. When he returned he had the blonde wig and the two photographs from his saddle pocket. He handed them to her, although it would probably distress her more when she studied the likenesses.

Sitting easily side by side, they examined them together, and Rudy explained how he had come by them. He remarked that Martha was like her mother. Eventually, an upsurge of emotion made further discussion for the girl more difficult.

"I don't think I'm very good company for you, Rudy. But you'll understand, I guess, seein' as how you know of my stepfather's death. My mother is buried quite close to this shack. I'll show you her grave in a little while.

"It was good of you to come. Really, it was. But I can't help you in your search for the murderer of Wil Haymes, an' I could never leave this valley — even if I wanted to — because of my brother, Dick. He suffered a loss of memory directly after that explosion on the railway. Since then, he's been unpredictable. He is aware of me, an' yet his memory is not restored. So the situation is hopeless for Dick an' me. An' you'll want to go on with your investigations elsewhere."

"It isn't hopeless, Martha," Rudy argued gently.

He stood up, stared out of the window again and was glad when she suggested that he should smoke, if he felt inclined. He did so, and presently he squatted on the tricky upright chair again.

"The situation is difficult, but not hopeless," he began again. "I've met Dick on two occasions. His memory is in much better fettle than you are aware of. I advised him to speak privately with you, about the prospect of seekin' your freedom. For both of you. So far, I reckon, he hasn't had the chance to contact you."

"That's true," Martha confirmed, keenly interested again. "As a matter of fact, he came into the valley a short while ago. I saw the wagon through the glass. Dick an' that bulky fellow, Ringo Spade. It seems the hawks may be gatherin' again. I don't like that Ringo jasper. And it all seems worse now, if, as you suggest, Dick has recovered his memory. I believe the Border gang want to start usin' him in one of their robberies."

Rudy paused in his pacing. "I'm glad you don't like Ringo. I have him as the prime suspect for the stabbin' of Wil Haymes."

This time Martha gasped, and clapped her hands to the sides of her head. "I always thought Ringo was real mean, but why would he kill Dick's stepfather? Did he know who it was?"

"Exactly why, I don't know yet. He was certainly close enough to Salt Creek to have done the murder. I think he believes Dick may inherit Haymes' money some day. Or share it with you. Perhaps he thought Haymes might recognize him from the attack on the railroad, or take Dick away with him. Alternatively, Haymes might have interrupted him when he was carryin' out a robbery, or goin' through Haymes' private belongings for information."

Martha shuddered. "It's all very involved and — and distasteful. Do you think Dick would quit travellin' with Spade, and dodge away from the gang, if he thought I was free and safe?"

"I'm sure he could be persuaded, Martha. You know this valley far better than I do. Is it possible to get out, intact, without goin' back up the obvious trail?"

"Just possible, I think," the girl surmised, furrowing her unlined brow. "It would mean avoidin' the look-outs down the creek, and being lucky, too. And once we moved we'd have to be prepared for anything. I owe such freedom as I've got here to Vegas Jack and no one else. Link Border and Deac Schmidt and the rest are pretty lethal. They don't share Spade's interest in my brother, Dick, to the same extent. Is there something I don't know about bothering you?"

"Yes, I guess there is. I talked with Ringo Spade down Saguaro way. If he knew I'd further contacted Dick, an' then turned up here, I'd be a marked man. A lot depends upon whether Vegas tells him about me, or whether there's a delay before the word goes around."

"Usually, the members of the gang, all but the leaders, make a camp out of doors beyond the stable," Martha explained. "I have this feeling they're grouping up for a big strike. Did you actually tell Vegas you were a peace officer?"

"Not in so many words," Rudy replied, after a pause, "but Spade will know the name. If they don't come lookin' for me real soon, I'd like to try an' get close to them unobserved, find out a bit more about their immediate plans. What do *you* think?"

Martha nodded, without enthusiasm. She had warmed to Rudy, but she doubted whether he could come and go unnoticed like she herself.

"Don't underestimate the lookouts, Rudy," she advised. "Go by dark, and don't take risks. Eh?"

Rudy was pleased by her apparent concern.

12

THE hours of early evening were eventful ones for Rudy and the girl he had so recently met. He found himself attracted to her in a way quite different from other western women he had known. She was pretty, strong, and mature for her age. Moreover, her costly upbringing in far-off Chicago had done nothing to spoil her. She knew the strengths and weaknesses of her kin, and her friends, too.

They dined off a succulent water-fowl roasted on a spit, helped down by small baked flour cakes and fruit. The coffee had never tasted better, and for a time Rudy shared the secure feeling which Martha experienced in regard to the island retreat. It was when they were relaxing beside the flickering outdoor fire, amid the deepening shadows, that the peace officer's nerves began to show again.

The frequent silences between them grew. At times, Rudy wished that all he had to do was smuggle her away: that Dick did not exist, and all he had to do was outwit a guard or two and spirit her away for himself. But, of course, it was not to be.

"If you are not back in a couple of hours, I'll come looking for you," Martha promised.

"Would that be wise, though?" Rudy argued. "If I was only delayed, you bein' away when I returned could ruin our plans. Better stay out of the action, Martha. Let me take tonight's risks."

Their faces were close, so that they could see each other's expressions in the fading light. It seemed natural when they kissed, and neither of them felt ill-at-ease or bashful. This time, Rudy took off his boots and waded across the fordable stretch. He had with him a Colt revolver, his Winchester, a spyglass and plenty of ammunition. No one apprehending him would ever believe that he was simply bird-watching. Soon, he was out of the water and drying his feet. Instead of boots he was about to wear moccasins provided by Martha for greater ease in the dark.

There was a healthy firelight glow coming from beyond the stables on the far side of the blockhouse accompanied by the sounds of men arguing and drinking. Ribald laughter was occasionally punctuated by the commanding high-pitched voice of Lincoln Border, their leader, although Marshal Girton, as he gradually wriggled closer, had no means of knowing his identity.

Not long after Rudy had started his lone furtive crawl, a pigeon flew away from Martha's islet and made its way with unerring accuracy to the lookout platform on top of the blockhouse. Scarcely had it cooed for more than a few seconds when the small figure of Delfina appeared at the top of the ladder and received the creature into her arms. For a few seconds, she cradled it, while her eyes were busy regarding the scene around the firelit camp. Her ears, too, picked up useful information, and by the time Vegas Jack stirred on his bunk she was by his side, unfolding the message which had been attached to the bird's leg.

Jack coughed, an innocent pipe-smoker's cough. "A message from Martha, is it, my little one? Read it to me. Quickly."

Delfina knelt beside him and quickly read the short note by the light of a flaring matchstick. She made an interested noise, and rubbed out the match. "She says her visitor is a good man. He believes Ringo Spade murdered her father in the town of Salt Creek. Also that her brother's memory is almost restored. The visitor wants her to escape with him. If he insists, she will agree. And this may be farewell, although she does not want to leave you."

Vegas sighed. He turned on his bunk, and patted Delfina's shoulder with tender affection. "Light me a pipe, Delfina. We must send a message back again. And burn the slip of paper which you hold, eh?"

The tiny Indian girl did as he had bidden her. They talked in whispers for a few minutes, and then the message was written out. Delfina wrote it in script, having been taught unjoined writing by her blind benefactor.

She then fed the bird, talked to it in whispers and took it up to the lookout loft. Her keen eyes noted its flight for quite a distance before the intervening trees screened it from view.

Rudy heard quite a few things which told him of the make-up of the outlaw gang: also that some of the lookouts had been pulled in to talk with the leader. However, when someone hurled a burning brand towards a bush where an owl was hooting, he knew he was in danger of being noticed, and that incident prompted him to back off and return to the creek island.

Martha called softly to him as he

waded through the last of the ford. His heart thumped with pleasure, rather than with shock. Soon, he was in the shack, sipping coffee and talking over his experience.

"Ringo an' Dick are in the valley, although I didn't actually see your brother. Also the leader, Link Border is there, with a man called Deacon Schmidt, and another called John."

Martha, kneeling beside him, nodded. "John Pilch. Also Ace Rammidge and Jimmy Volk, back from Arroyo. And some of the lookouts have been pulled in for a special discussion. There is to be a strike against a bank, but it is not clear where."

Rudy discarded his cup, and gently gripped her by the shoulders.

"You know more than I do about what is goin' on, Martha. How is that possible?"

The girl chuckled, and kissed him lightly on the lips. "I sent a message to the blockhouse by pigeon. Delfina is a very good scholar. She read it to

Jack, and he composed a message for the reply. He says that if I am to go it ought to be done immediately, because the hawks are getting ready for another strike. Where the strike is to be is not clear. Perhaps in Arroyo, or some place further east."

Rudy went to the door and studied the distant stars. Martha quickly joined him. He said: "Immediately, eh? Would you go tonight, while some of the lookouts are away from their posts?"

"With you, yes. If you will take my advice, Rudy."

He embraced her and whispered in her ear. "I feel I have known you for a long time. Ever since I first saw your photograph. The feeling is a kind of magic."

"I feel it, as well," Martha assured him. "We will travel light. There is one lookout on the north side of the creek, in the direction we must take. He has the sharpened senses of an animal, but we can outwit him. Between us."

With their arms linked across their

backs, they sauntered back into the shack. Martha had a plan, and Rudy was keen to hear it.

* * *

There was no ford to speak of on the north side of the creek isle. Rudy therefore took it upon himself to swim to the mainland with most of his clothing in a bundle just clear of the water. In the last few yards a faint tremor of fear went through him as his keen eyes studied the high ground back from the bank.

His adversary was a man in a coonskin cap with a formidable reputation as a trapper of animals and a killer of men. This fellow had a whole string of crimes behind him, which meant it was safer to be well away from the ordinary haunts of men. He could live in the wild and not feel deprived. He of all the lookouts was the only one to live in a dugout, constructed by himself.

Time-worn stones indicated to Rudy

that he was almost over. He kept low and slowly emerged, hugging the roots of the nearest trees, and hoping to stay unobserved. The dugout was supposed to be a few hundred feet above the creek and to the right. Rudy hoped that the lookout was not on an all-night fishing expedition, or taking a distant view up the valley towards the blockhouse.

Quite soon he had dried himself and donned his denims and shirt. The exertion made him breathless, and a certain tension added to his breathing difficulties. In three minutes he stumbled into a dry ditch which marked the lower end of a gentle rounded ridge which curved up the hill. After pausing for breath, he crossed over the ridge, which was no more than a couple of paces across at the base, and began a slow, cautious ascent of the other side.

A rock fault, like a miniature pass, came up quite quickly, and Rudy paused there with the first part of the plan completed. No more than two minutes elapsed when the sound of a night bird floated up from the island. The distinctive call was repeated, and a brief light showed: a masked lantern, in the hands of Martha.

A man with a husky voice cleared his throat. He emerged from the very soil, so it seemed, no more than a hundred feet away. Rudy held his breath. A match-stick rasped into light. A brightness shone through chinks in the roof of the dugout, and a truly bright light briefly transformed the hillside as the door opened and closed.

The intruder found himself flexing his toes in the borrowed moccasins. The lookout also wore moccasins, but he was intent upon a new arrival from the island, rather than anyone closer at hand.

The guard passed by without glancing at the hiding-place. He moved down the slope, surefooted, even in the dark.

On the isle, Martha came through the trees on the back of her horse, a dappled grey gelding. She appeared to have donned a cloak, and was carrying a lamp in her right hand. Rudy was thankful that her presence was so obvious. It would hold the guard's attention as well as his own.

Eventually, Rudy plucked up enough courage to quit his hiding-place and follow the guard. He had to give so much attention to the uneven going under foot that he would have been detected had not Martha been down there as the focus of attention.

Although it did not move very rapidly, the creek water tended to muffle other sounds from the ears of anyone close to the bank. Nearer and nearer went the two men, one seeing all the movement, and the other intent upon the woman and the swimming grey horse. In the last few yards before they came together, Martha must have clearly seen her ally, as he rose to his full height, holding a small rock in his right hand.

She checked the grey, and called for

assistance. The man in the coonskin hat muttered something and stepped into the shallows with a hand outstretched. Rudy hit him then. The stone connected with his head, which would have been badly bruised, but for the fur hat.

The guard slumped, made an effort to recover and then lost consciousness. Between them they hauled him ashore again. Rudy stood over him, while Martha dismounted. Her night vision was good, and she proceeded with the trussing, using some special leather thongs which she had brought with her.

Rudy gave a personal whistle, and stood like a statue for a few seconds, wondering if his dun horse would answer the summons and cross the water. The suspense faded as it whinnied. He called encouragingly to it and saw it plunge into the water.

"There's no going back now, Rudy," Martha murmured, as she rose from her knees. "He won't take any harm there, as the night is mild. We should be moving on, though, as soon as possible, so if you want to swop your boots for the moccasins, go ahead."

The victim groaned, but he was far from regaining consciousness. Rudy had wiped down the dun and was ready to ride in a little over ten minutes. This time, Martha took the initiative, guiding her stumbling mount up the lower side of the ridge and moving slowly but surely in an easterly direction. Soon, they were round a curve in the creek. Some of the stiffness went out of Rudy, who found himself wondering how much time they had in hand before daybreak.

On they went, adjusting to the uneven undulating track, and gradually putting distance between themselves and the outlaw-controlled valley. The dun trudged along behind the grey gelding, and for quite a while Girton was content to fix his tired eyes on the slim figure it carried.

There was little room for contentment in his mind, and yet he had achieved something. He had found Martha, and he had brought her out of the vale-of-no-return. Even though she had done most of the scheming. He smiled broadly. His expression remained that way, but his body slumped in the saddle.

★ ★ ★

A change in the motion failed to rouse him, but the clatter of horseshoes on timber logs did. He blinked himself awake, and found the grey a couple of yards away, facing towards him. Martha's tired face looked a little on the tense side, but she was still able to smile. There was something special in her expression which he knew was only for him.

"Howdy, Rudy, welcome to a new day. I'm glad you awakened yourself, 'cause we have to make a decision. A man's decision, I figure. This contraption we're standing on is an old raft ferry. It hasn't been used for a year or two. The landing-spot on the other side of the creek was washed away when the river was in spate."

"I remember," Rudy replied, nodding vigorously. "An' if we can get it movin' again we can make better progress. At least as far as the next settlement, which I believe is called East Ferry. Am I right?"

"You are right, *amigo*, and the dawn is about half an hour away. So what do you think our chances are?"

Rudy felt his chin stubble with his finger-tips. He wanted to show up well in front of his new girlfriend, for whom he had accepted responsibility. He knew the chances of moving the raft without help were no better than fifty-fifty.

"I don't know, Martha, but if you take the horses right forward an' get them to prance about a little I may be able to ease the stern end off the sand and mud. We'll give it a try."

So saying, he dismounted and handed his reins over to his partner. Martha accepted them and coaxed the two uncertain horses to the forward end of the raft. In the centre of it was a shelter of sorts amounting to wooden walls to chest height. As a shelter from the elements it was a failure, but it might have provided a modicum of safety from flying arrows a few decades earlier.

Rudy hurled aside the plank at the rear, dismantled the long stern steering-oar and manipulated it in such a way that it could be used as a lever. At first, the pressure he used failed to move the raft, but the animals thumped about quite a bit and Martha called some encouragement.

"Keep trying, Rudy, you never know. Don't strain yourself, though. How would it be if I came down there and hung on the pole with you?"

Rudy heaved again. He opened his mouth to answer Martha, but just as he did so she leapt down to the boards. A slithering noise followed her descent, and no further discussion was necessary. Panting for breath, Rudy managed to keep the logs moving. After that, it was a frantic scramble to get on board without having to get wet again.

He contrived to make contact with the stern end. Between them, they heaved the steering-oar back into place, and then they were out in midstream. Martha attended to the steering, while Rudy stripped off the saddles and blankets. They watched each other, eyes heavy through lack of sleep, and pleased nevertheless with their achievements so far.

Soon, the dun and the grey were secured to ringbolts in the superstructure, and their condition improved due to the grooming, even if they were hungry for worthwhile fodder.

When Rudy took over the oar and advised Martha to get between the walls and sleep, his brow was furrowed. "Hey, Martha, how long is it since we first met? Do you have any idea?"

Even though she had dark smudges

under her eyes, the girl still looked pretty when she flashed her teeth in a smile. "Why, that was a lifetime ago, mister. Fancy you not remembering."

The raft was not difficult to steer. The banks sped by without incident, the changing scenes making life difficult for the weary steersman. Before the sun became really hot, he contrived to clean his revolver and Winchester. Sooner or later the two of them would be in use, and the difference between life and death was often reduced simply to timing and efficiency.

He wondered how keen the Border gang would be in trying to get Martha back into their clutches. Obviously, she knew too much about their private arrangements for going to ground. Would they send a team after her, or would they wait until after the next strike against a bank?

And what about her brother, Dick? Had he as much spirit as his sister, or had his courage permanently ebbed since the explosion had affected his memory? How strong was the bond between Martha and Dick?

Rudy knew he had a lot to learn about this brother and sister relationship. He had achieved a lot in locating them, but he was still a long way from getting his man, and from thwarting the Border gang in its latest exploits. Sam Callaway and their temporary change of roles seemed way back in the past, but Sam had suffered at the hands of this mob, and Rudy had to strike back on Sam's behalf if the chance presented itself.

He was scowling and deep in thought when he noticed an old shingle nailed to a tree. It indicated that the township of East Ferry was not more than a mile downstream.

13

RUDY parked the raft in a convenient inlet about one thousand yards short of the township. It was sufficiently secluded not to be noticed by picnickers, or people on casual horse-riding jaunts in search of the wide-open spaces.

All the obvious traffic was on the side to the south, and even there fifty yards of thick scrub and trees separated passers-by from the water. This meant that the inlet — on the north side — was not overlooked from the outer bank.

All that day they slept, taking turns to watch every two hours. Through the night the watches were extended to four hours. Fortunately, Martha had packed quite a few provisions in her saddlebags, and she had the knack of making a meal out of next to nothing.

During the following forenoon Rudy saddled up and rode a short way to the north, seeking high points in the terrain from which he could study the lie of the land to eastward and westward.

While he was using the glass in one spot, a big old cart with a grinding wheel needing oil started to come from Colorado and the north. Girton moved back onto the trail and passed the time of day with the farmer and his family who were intent upon seeking new pastures nearer the border with Mexico.

He rode along beside them for a short distance, and took an interest in the stores they had, which would be replenished in East Ferry. Eventually, he bought up flour, bacon and other items which they were eager to part with, and thus purchased more time before he was compelled to go into town for essential supplies.

Martha complimented him upon his forethought, but she was becoming restless. During the midday meal they argued without heat.

"Sooner or later we have to take a look at the town," the girl pointed out. "Either we find enemies there, or we don't. If we don't, then we have to plan some more. I'll take a look myself, if you like."

Rudy, slightly displeased, hurriedly denied her the privilege.

"Oh no, I'll make the first visit. I reckon it's man's work, an' you won't argue about that. I'm not keen on the two of us partin', but I think it's for the best, at the outset. When do you suggest I go?"

"Later today?" Martha suggested gently.

She had intended to add, in the evening when the shadows provided cover of a sort, but Rudy had other ideas.

"All right, this afternoon. When most of the folks will be takin' a siesta. *That's* when I'll go. Besides, darkness could bring a sneak attack on the raft, here, if the outlaws were around."

Rudy washed the dishes in the creek and generally tidied up. It was his intention to take a brief nap in the long grass before heading for town. He found Martha in their private quarters, surrounded by plaited tall grass. She had combed out her plaits and was in the process of tying back her long locks at the nape of her neck. She used the black silk neck-band, which she wore to remind her of her mother's death. Rudy fixed it in a broad bow.

Then, as she knelt near him, she undid a fine gold chain from her neck and showed him a small picture of her mother, Juliana.

"I want you to take this with you, Rudy. Wear it like I've always done."

Two small tears escaped down her cheeks. Rudy gently brushed them away and shook his head. "I know how much you miss your mother. It was clear when we stood together by her grave, on the island."

"Take it, just the same. As a token of what I feel for you. Besides, if you meet Dick he will know that he can trust you. It will help him to go along with any plans you may have for the future."

Rudy gave in, slowly and gravely. He counselled her not to be other than vigilant while he was away, and left hurriedly, foregoing his short siesta and contenting himself with a few kisses and a loving hug, which said a great deal.

* * *

Nothing happened on the way in to disturb his outward calm. East Ferry was just like any other western town at mid-afternoon in the hot season. A few bodies sprawled here and there, some sleeping off alcohol, others merely speeding the heat of the day on its way, preferring the cool of the evening.

Dogs lolled about dry-tongued and panting. The blinds and drapes were down in some of the choosier shops. Mounted up, Rudy made a tour of the streets, two or three deep in an obvious grid. About twenty minutes after his arrival he walked the dun round the vacant lots at the back of Lincoln Avenue and edged it into the shade of the alley alongside a smart barber's shop.

Right opposite, across the avenue, was the Ford Hotel: a neat two-storey building painted white. Next in line was the Ferryman's bank, which had an imposing frontage, a false balcony above the entrance and a flat roof with a big name-board fixed to it in a vertical position.

Rudy yawned. He decided that Lincoln Avenue was a messy thoroughfare. With an effort he kept his thoughts from slipping back to Martha, and went to work on what his next move ought to be.

Consequently, he had stared at the parked cart with the faded patched canvas for quite a while before its significance dawned upon him. It had been temporarily lodged in front of the hotel. The horses which normally pulled it had been freed. At that very moment their necks were stretched over a wooden water-trough in the rear of the cart. Chestnut horses, broad in the beam. Familiar horses, too!

Rudy was so shocked he gasped. He was actually staring at the travelling wagon belonging to Ringo Spade and Dick van Groot! At last, his wayward eyes turned in the direction of the palatial barber's shop. Before the barber took over it had been a fine dress shop, with a wide display crescent of window looking onto the street.

Now, the barber had his chairs facing towards the street, so that his clients could watch the townsfolk and vehicles going and coming while their beards were trimmed and their hair was cut. Two chairs were occupied, side by side. Disembodied heads peered street-wards from over protective cloths. The barber and his chief assistant were busy with their razors. Soap gave way before the blades, revealing hairless sunburned skin.

Feeling as if his chest muscles had seized up on him, Rudy struggled to cope with more tension than he could ever remember.

Neither Ringo nor Dick happened to be looking straight towards the hotel, and their wagon parked in front of it. Each of them was closely studying the impressive frontage of the Ferryman's bank, the next building further down the street on the opposite side.

All kinds of warring thoughts sped through the town marshal's mind. His eyes photographed on his memory two hitch-rails, the short flight of steps up to the front entrance, the twin windows, one on either side, both painted into opaqueness in their lower halves, and the apparent thickness of the twin doors.

He forced himself to breath deeply and slowly. Then, lowering his head, he dismounted, putting the dun's body between him and the formidable profile of Ringo Spade. Perspiration oozed from his forehead and body. As he hazarded a sharp glance across the saddle another development occurred.

A man on a spritely pinto horse had come from the left. The rider in question, a tall lean man, wearing a coonskin hat, checked the two-tone horse, grinned tightly and deliberately gave his attention to the barber's window. He recognized the pair in the chairs, although neither of them showed the slightest interest in him.

Emitting a dry, wicked chuckle, the newcomer dismounted, licking his lips in anticipation. He slackened his saddle-girth with a muscular arm, and heaved the sweating animal towards the trough and between the chestnut shaft horses.

At the same time, Rudy turned his horse about, keeping his head down, and directed it up the alley, away from the danger spot. On the vacant lot behind the barber's and the tailor's shop next door, he tethered the dun to a clothes-post, and hurriedly took stock of what he knew. How could he turn to advantage his knowledge of the three men's presence? Every time he thought of the man he had left trussed up near the water he perspired afresh. Obviously, he had not suffered unduly from the blow on the head. Here he was, contacting other gang members in East Ferry. But what about? The intense interest of both Ringo and Dick suggested a raid on the bank, not merely a chase after an elusive girl and an interfering peace officer . . .

★ ★ ★

In the barber's shop the powerful personality of the man in the skin hat had an effect upon the barbers. Clancy hovered in front of the pair in the chairs until Ringo noticed him.

"Hold it, barber. I got to talk with my friend, here."

Ringo snapped his fingers in the direction of Dick, who immediately became embarrassed and started to wipe the residue of soap from his face with the protecting cloth. One barber indicated a third, empty chair, but Ringo would have none of it.

"Dick, you're finished or as near as done. Go an' get yourself a drink, why don't you? Clancy and me, we'll catch up with you in a few minutes."

Dick allowed his barber to remove the cover from his shoulders and accepted a damp face-cloth with which he cleaned up his jowls.

"Okay, Ringo, if that's what you want," he replied, hesitantly.

He backed out of the door on the east side of the shop, with Ringo's offer to pay his bill ringing in his ears. Next beyond the tailor's was Melindy's Restaurant, and Melindy herself was a pretty young woman in her early thirties. Before Dick could set out for refreshment, Rudy Girton sprang into view at the rear of the barber's, signalled for him to remain calm, and then hurried to meet him.

Dick felt nervous, as he received yet another shock. Here was the fellow who was interested in his sister, in fact all the family. Life surely was getting complicated. In a way, It was easier to manage when his memory was still faulty.

Rudy gripped him by the hand, shook it warmly, and drew him to one side. "Howdy, Dick, things are happening. Martha is no longer in the valley. I have her in a safe place. The gang is plannin' a strike against the bank. Right? That's serious, but it may be your chance to break away an' return to an honest way of living. Martha would want that, wouldn't she?"

Dick was licking his lips and starting to shake his head. Rudy slapped him on the shoulder and, remembering about the photo in the locket, he undid his bandanna and showed the precious memento to the startled youth.

"Martha gave me this to show you. So you'd know I spoke the truth, see? Make your way to the nearest saloon, an' come back with two tall glasses of beer. Do it as quickly as you can. I'll be waitin' for you here. Don't ask questions. Do it. You have money?"

With an effort, Dick managed to get his troubled thoughts in order. He had *dinero*, and he signified that he was ready to go along with Rudy's instructions. He went off, bursting with scarcely-suppressed excitement. Meanwhile, Rudy sidled closer to the shop.

The barbers had tactfully removed themselves into the back room while the short conference took place. Ringo had removed his cloth and was smoking, still sitting in the big chair. Clancy had taken off his fur hat and was skilfully snipping off bits of his own hair, watching his image in the mirror.

"Link sure enough ain't pleased about the girl makin' off with that tricky hombre who asked to see her. Neither am I, for that matter. If I see him again, I'm goin' to kill him. But about tomorrow. The meeting's at two o'clock, right? The Boss approves of you usin' the boy as a horse-minder. If he looks at all doubtful, shoot him. You go along with that, Ringo? Any of the other details we discussed in camp that don't seem right?"

"Not that I can see, Clancy," Ringo returned easily. It had never been his intention to involve Dick, but if Border saw it that way he was not going to argue. "You know where we'll be until the time comes. And what follows after. Any sign of the girl yet?"

"None at all, but she's bound to show up, sooner or later. When this caper is over I'm goin' to make it my business to find out where she went, an' how."

Dick's heavy breathing startled Rudy, who backed away from his listening-post and rejoined him further down the alley. Young van Groot had carried out Rudy's instruction to the letter, not pausing to get a drink for himself. He had slopped out a small amount of beer from each glass, otherwise the two offerings were intact.

"They hit the bank at two tomorrow. Me, I've got to contact one or two friends. I want you to be on the alert tomorrow. You're involved. Right? As a horse-minder. I'll be around. If things go well you could back me up. That way, you'd help both Martha an' me. Remember, I'm Martha's protector. She'd want you to try, even if it was risky. Why don't you go down there to the shop? Sit on the step outside, as if you were waitin' permission to go in. You could hear something important before they notice you. I've got to clear out real soon. I'll tell Martha you're fit an' ready an' willin'. Keep on the alert. *Hasta la vista!*"

Rudy hurried away.

Dick called after him: "Be seein' you, Rudy!"

His dry-throated call sounded like desperation. Rudy collected the dun and mounted up, putting a couple of blocks between himself and the two watchful outlaws in the barber's shop.

He had no idea if Dick would back him the following day. Nor did he have much confidence in the outcome of tomorrow's clash. A half-hour later he called at the telegraph office.

His first message was addressed to the county sheriff in the county seat, Piute Junction.

It said: *Join me at Ferryman's two o'clock tomorrow bring the boys.* Signed: *Callaway*.

The other was addressed to the town marshal of Salt Creek City, and read: *Shindig at Ferryman's two o'clock tomorrow boys from Piute expected regards Rudy*.

Rudy went all the way into the office and round the back of the counter. The hook-nosed clerk, blinking under his eye-shade, tensed up at first. Girton let him feel the shape of his star through the cloth of his pocket. After that the clerk's attitude changed. Two silver dollars changed hands, over and above the cost of the transmissions. The eye-shade was lifted.

"I've heard of you, Mr Callaway. Always thought you was older, though. I'll send these straight away. Important, are they?"

"Very important, my friend. If you keep their contents a secret you could come into a small amount of money tomorrow. Understand?"

The clerk made the sign of a cross on his shiny waistcoat. Rudy patted him on the shoulder encouragingly and left him, but he stayed close. For over an hour the determined peace officer kept a watch on the office. Nothing happened to make him think the clerk would double-cross him.

Eventually, tiredness and a burning desire to be back in Martha's company before the action started forced him to leave. He took every precaution on the way out, other than riding back to front in the saddle. He saw none of the gang. No one followed him.

14

GIRTON moseyed back into town in the hour before noon on the critical day. Instead of thinking forward to the coming action, his thoughts were busy with his latest session in the company of Martha.

He had found her well, and anxious to have him restored to her. The evening had passed pleasantly for them, the couple needing no other company, but in the night the pressure of what lay ahead brought Rudy out in perspiration. He awoke struggling, fighting off enemies — so he thought — only to find that in his ramblings he had awakened Martha, and that it was she who struggled with him, trying to calm him down.

She had bathed his head with a damp cloth and talked soothingly for a long time about her childhood to distract from his current worries. After her treatment he had slept better, and she had been the first to awaken in the hour after dawn.

They shared the chores, and both ate well. After breakfast he went over all that he had done the previous day, in town, including all the details about his encounter with Dick. To pass on a little more time in the forenoon they bathed in the creek and splashed each other like youngsters on a day's outing.

Inevitably, the parting-time had come around and left them short of apt things to say. Martha had a fob watch which had belonged to her mother. By referring to it, she hoped to roughly keep track of the developments in town.

When Rudy finally saddled up and left, she ran up and down the slope back from the creek-side to catch the very last possible glimpse of him as he went out of sight.

All the way into town he behaved as if every bush, every stone, was observing him. It only wanted a small thing to go wrong for the outlaws to become warned that someone was wise to their plan.

A few riders and freighter drivers went by in the other direction, quitting town for locations further north and west. Perhaps twice as many filtered into town. The newcomers were moving more slowly, having done a lot of riding or driving in the preceding days.

East Ferry absorbed them. No one paid a lot of heed to newcomers, except for the unemployed who mooched about in the shade, flopped on the sidewalk benches, and watched the new arrivals in the hope that there was a soft touch on the way in.

Every small consideration was a problem of sorts. Like where to leave the dun so as not to have it in an obvious spot . . . By riding slowly down a back street he solved that one. A plump widow was seated on the sill of a first-floor window, cleaning the pane of glass. Her shack and the one next to it had a communal grass patch, half turf and half paddock.

When Rudy reined in and cocked a leg around his saddle-horn their eyes met. She read his thoughts. He touched his hat, surveying the backs of other properties and weighing up the accessibility of the private patch.

"If you figure on leavin' it for a few hours it'll be all right. It looks like it's ready for a rest, anyways. You slacken off that saddle. Leave a dollar in the pocket, an' I'll give him a rub down soon as I've finished the windows. All right?"

"All right, ma'am, that'll suit me fine. Glad I ran across you. Kind of warm for the time of the mornin', ain't it?"

She was happy to chat him up for as long as he wanted; also to abandon her work and make him a drink of coffee, but his pressing worries would not let him unwind altogether. He made his excuses, reckoned he'd be back in the afternoon, and scowled as he reflected that his return was not an absolute certainty.

The only surprise the widow showed was when he lovingly removed his Winchester from the saddle scabbard and checked over the basic functions of his Colt six-shooter. She was worldly enough to know what he was doing when he made a furtive check of the spare ammunition he was carrying.

"Don't go robbin' any banks is all I ask!"

Her voice floated down to him as she wriggled seductively back into her bedroom and eased down the sash window, which squeaked.

Three separate times he squatted down on an unoccupied bench and lowered the Winchester butt to the boards. Ever since the widow saw him unload it he had been more than passing conscious of its significance.

At half-past one he approached the area of the bank, the Ford Hotel and other buildings familiar from the day before. As soon as he paused near the barber's shop, he felt too conscious of his own presence. The Border gang were very thorough. They would almost certainly have one of their number keeping watch on the bank, and the approaches to it.

He wanted to march straight up the low flight of steps and into the bank, but his shoulder weapon would at once have drawn attention to him. Customers and bank-tellers would all have reacted suspiciously, and that would never do. He sighed, kept his head down, studied the strolling public on all sides — tormenting himself with the possibilities — and then stepped forward.

He gave ground to a buckboard with a lively ex-cavalry officer holding the reins, ducked a bulky rider with a side-stepping skewbald horse, and then he was through the traffic, stepping with shoulders hunched along the alley between the Ford Hotel and the bank.

An unruly part of his mind made him wonder exactly what Martha was doing at that very moment. He blinked as he recollected seeing her fix a small Derringer pistol under the broad garter, quite high on a very shapely thigh.

The butt of the Winchester clanged against a trash-can, and that brought him back to the present. He flinched, in case anyone came out to see what was happening. No one did. Around the back of the bank the shutters were neatly painted. He surmised quite correctly that he was outside the room of the manager or president.

What to do now? He got as far as the rear door, thought about knocking on it, and then changed his mind. Instead, he lowered the Winchester down beside the wall, left it there, and completed his circuit of the building. Still no obvious signs of trouble.

The thumping of his heart prevented him from procrastinating any longer. Up the steps, stumbling without cause, and into the building. The interior showed signs of prosperity. The public section went back about two-thirds of the depth of the building. The big counter with the tellers' positions was on the right with the usual ironwork protection flanking the grilles. The door to the president's room was right forward, with a spreading pot-plant on either hand.

Over on the left was a similar space to the right, but it was given over to customers. No counter there, but a long padded bench and a couple of plush armchairs. An oil-painting of a western round-up graced the wall between the big chairs.

Three customers were idling about near two of the grilles. A plump elderly settler, probably a German or a Dutch farmer, fully filled one armchair, while his thin gaunt wife was poised uncomfortably on the end of the bench.

The customers glanced at Rudy and immediately lost interest. He touched his hat to anyone who was anticipating such a move and strode across to the president's door. At once the youthful teller whose position was not occupied protested. "Sir, I'd like to help you. I'm sure I could. Only Mr Freeman the president, don't take kindly to visitors in the afternoon, 'specially if they happen to be strangers."

Rudy halted, stepped back a pace and crooked his index finger a few times. Very reluctantly the nervous youth came from behind the counter and hovered behind the intruder. Rudy set his teeth, wondered what he should do for the best, and finally came up with an idea.

He used his badge again. After palming it, he forced the young teller to shake hands. The pointed shape of the star made its impression upon his palm. Clearly, he received the message which Rudy intended.

"You can listen at the door, if you don't like this. If you decide to go up town for your own peace officer, mind how you go. The building is almost certainly under observation right now."

Rudy nodded and grinned, and from thenceforth ignored him.

He knocked, opened the door, excused himself to a Mr Freeman he had not yet seen, and stepped inside. The double-width desk was very imposing, located as it was directly in front of the communicating door. A big window was half-way along the outer wall, behind the desk. At the left-hand end was a smaller room with a washroom sign on it. At the other end was a cloakroom which gave access to the rear outside door.

The great safe was against the outer wall to the left of the desk. In a similar position to the right was a massive filing cabinet. President Freeman already suffered with high blood pressure. When he was angry, his chief irritant was being ignored. He moved his florid face this way and that, trying to transfix Rudy with non-steely bloodshot eyes.

"You want to take over the bank now, or will tomorrow do?"

Rudy felt easier now that he was indoors and in a position to plan a few details. He tossed his stetson on the desk, scoring a bull on the brand-new blotter.

"Howdy, Mr Freeman. The Border gang is goin' to hit your bank in force in just a few minutes. I'm the town marshal of Salt Creek. You can believe me or not, as you wish. If you stay you will probably die in here. Too late to make a new will. I did my best yesterday to encourage back-up from out of town. Maybe it will come too late. Tell you what you'll do. Catfoot out of the back door. Head for the marshal's office without drawin' attention to yourself. Tell him what I've told you. Bring as many guns as he can find. Pronto."

Freeman waved a shaking fist, shaken but not convinced, and extremely angry. A heavy cough in the other room drew Rudy to the communicating door. He placed his ear to it. Freeman's protest faded. Only anxiety held his

231

features after that. Rudy waved him away, and this time he grabbed his silk hat and headed for the cloakroom door.

"Mr Freeman, hand in my Winchester before you go. It's against the rear wall, outside."

Acting on impulse, Rudy followed the president out of doors and took a quick look up the passage. Three determined-looking men were approaching the bank on horseback from the east. His mind was so sharp that he identified two of them from reward notices seen in Salt Creek months earlier.

Link Border and his right-hand man, Deacon Schmidt. The other could conceivably be John Pilch; a white man with a bronzed tint to his skin, wearing a coarse dark woollen cloak and an undented black hat.

Freeman ran away, round the backs of the buildings. Rudy stopped being a statue and ran round the back again. He danced on past, and squinted up the other alley. There, he froze again.

232

Ringo Spade had just dismounted out front, and was in the act of handing over his reins.

The voice carried. "Now keep all these cayuses together, Dick. Here, by the rail. If anybody looks like interfering while we're inside, do something about it. The horse-minder in an outfit like this is a key figure."

Dick van Groot, just out of sight from the alley, must have agreed. Gasping with relief, Rudy danced back out of sight. In a second or two he was back in the rear office, holding his Winchester like a club. He propped it against the desk, and checked the office again. Someone was bound to investigate the big safe. Surprise might help. He crossed to a tall cupboard, built like a wardrobe.

There was room for him inside. He stepped in, hatless, and pulled the doors until they were nearly closed . . .

★ ★ ★

233

Border, Schmidt, Clancy and Spade went in together, as couples. Spreading out, they all four pulled up identical bandannas from their necks. The similarity was in colour. All of them were cream.

The thin woman on the bench was the first to scream. Her stout husband dropped to the ground and reduced his bulk sufficiently to hide behind his chair.

Border remarked: "Right, folks, you've guessed it. This is a hold-up. Link Border an' friends officiating. Movement an' noise lead to casualties."

By this time eight revolvers were menacing the tellers, the customers and the pair just in for a rest. Clancy stood out from the others on account of his skin cap. He drew a shot from the most courageous of the tellers. At once, Clancy fired back. His bullet flew off the ironwork. Two guns fired at the armed teller, who went down, seriously wounded, but not before he had fired another bullet at Clancy and hit him in the head. Clancy flopped on hands and knees, fatally hit in the head, in a position to watch his life-blood dripping away.

"All right, hold it! It was a mistake on our part to shoot!"

The voice came from behind the counter. From an absolute bedlam of indoor firing, the shooting suddenly stopped. Poised like a ballet dancer, Link Border weighed up the situation, his dark calculating eyes taking in everything over his mask. His brows were like black bars, in contrast to his grey temples.

"Out in front! All of you! Do it now!"

All hands this time were raised. Out came the two fit tellers, fumbling up the counter-flap, their startled eyes going this way and that. Deacon Schmidt, his fleshy face beaded with sweat under the Quaker hat, dug them all in the back with a revolver barrel as they emerged and helped them to lie down without delay. As Clancy flattened out on the floor, Schmidt pushed his bulk through the flap and headed for the safe, which was open.

"Try the back room, Ringo!"

Border's voice sounded like a hiss behind his mask. Spade murmured his approval and headed for the president's door . . .

* * *

Three bullets, fired for effect, came through the woodwork of the communicating door near the lock and handle. Ringo Spade erupted into the room, sprang forward a yard to be on the safe side, and found it apparently empty. The deep-set crafty eyes swivelled this way and that in the narrow space between the cream bandanna and the bony forehead. His breathing eased, and his attention focused on the safe. He put down one of his twin guns to try the lock.

At the same time, Rudy kicked open

the two doors of his cupboard and blasted off two bullets, his left hand supporting his right as he fired. One hit Spade in the neck. The other penetrated the left side of his chest as his body was thrown back against the wall. The outlaw clawed his mask off his face, and fell forwards, crawling in the direction of the desk. He discarded his other revolver, which had suddenly grown heavy, and felt for a throwing-knife at his belt.

The second bullet had done more damage than he at first thought. It slowed him at once. He rolled over, gritting his teeth, and brought up his knees with the onset of pain and difficult breathing.

Rudy ducked down and went towards him on all fours, stripping him of his knife, and sharing his attention between his victim and the door through to the front. The bagging of money was going on in there. After the shooting in the back room, a bullet came through the door, high up in a panel. There was a hoarse shout, but no immediate development.

The policeman in Rudy came uppermost for a brief spell. "Ringo, why did you knife Wilbur Haymes?"

Spade sweated and fought for a little more time. "I ... knew ... who ... he was. Wanted to know ... more. He ... surprised me. I ... reacted. Didn't want him ... to link up ... with Dick again."

He gathered himself for another effort, but his wounds proved too much for him. His eyes flickered. He gave a wry grin, the friendliest expression Rudy had ever seen on his face, and expired. As the huge head rolled lifeless on the bulky shoulders, two hand-guns pumped bullets into the communicating door.

At the same time John Pilch, who had been guarding the front steps, stepped indoors and surveyed the scene in the tellers' room. Having almost tripped over the thin woman, he recovered himself, noted Clancy's inert body,

238

and looked for Ringo. Border, himself, who had been firing at the middle door, sprang round to face him and only just managed to hold his fire. The strain was telling upon their nerves.

Pilch shouted hoarsely. "Time's gettin' on, Boss! What happened to Ringo?"

Border pointed to the back room. Pilch licked his lips. "You need a shield of some sort, Boss!"

"You're right!" Border gasped. "Push the stout hombre over here, an' back me up!"

The skinny woman fainted as her husband assumed a bigger part in the lethal action.

15

AFTER the shooting at the middle door, the ensuing silence was almost unbearable. Border's breath was rasping in his throat as he pushed the reluctant farmer in front of him. He paused a yard away from the splintered door, no doubt thinking of Ringo Spade's fate.

"Deac, do you have those three money-bags filled yet."

"Sure, Boss," came the reply from behind the counter. "Largely coins and notes of small value."

Schmidt meant that they had not really amassed a large amount of loot. He was hinting that the big stuff was probably in the president's room. Growing anxiety in case they stayed too long prevented him from being more explicit.

Close behind the short stout farmer,

Border muttered: "I'm goin' to kick the door in. You duck a little an' keep on movin' forward! Make sure whoever is in there sees you, then he won't shoot you! Understand?"

The bullet-head bobbed, and Border had gathered himself when Schmidt called out from near the window, behind the counter.

"Hey, Boss, that young jasper, van Groot! Guess what? He's shifted the horses away from the rail! He ain't wearin' his mask, either! He's moved 'em over there, in the alley beside the barber's!"

Schmidt's voice had risen to a near crescendo. Rudy Girton, keyed up and ready, caught the gist of what he was saying through a splintered hole in the middle door. The peace officer let out his breath in a sigh of relief. Dick had not let him down. Young van Groot had put himself in a situation of considerable danger. These fleeting thoughts, and others, coursed through his mind as he waited for the next challenge. No local assistance. No sounds of a posse from out of town. Only Dick fighting the battle with him, and the risks were still greatly stacked against them.

Martha. Martha? That sweet girl? One he intended to spend his life with, if he had the chance. How could he face Martha again if her brother, Dick, was killed? The idea appalled him. Obviously, he — Rudy — had been responsible for making Dick change sides. Dick was his responsibility. Rudy groaned, and waited.

* * *

Dick, himself, was in a nervous state. Mindful of his need to take the pressures off Rudy Girton, he lined up his rifle from the barber's alley and pumped four bullets through the huge panes of glass. Two on the left, and two on the right. And then he paused.

He was reasoning that Rudy must be still alive, otherwise Border, Schmidt and the others would long since have been out, shouting for the horses and spraying lead this way and that. His mind clung to the idea that Ringo was in there, too. He knew Ringo would not hesitate to shoot at him, if he had to, but could he — Dick — blast the man who had shown him some kindness, even if that kindness was for the wrong sort of reason?

Alternately licking and biting his lips, he studied the alley, the restless horses, the empty frontage of the bank and hotel, the barren sidewalk. If they came for him and the horses his chances of survival would be low. A second glance in the reverse direction gave him a glimmer of hope. A flight of wooden stairs, going up the side of the tailor's building onto the flat roof. If he watched from up there he could be in a commanding position. Safer, too. The seconds dragged by. Waiting was foolish. So, he crouched lower, turned his back on the nervous horses and started up the staircase.

* * *

The delay did not do Rudy's nerves any good at all. It had him weighing the possibilities of dashing out by the back door and attempting to renew the fight from the front steps. Fortunately, perhaps, he did not have to make such a move.

Two more bullets further gouged holes in the shattered door. Border's boot hit it, and it gave at once, shuddering and swinging open. Forward went the unfortunate farmer, with the outlaw leader just a foot or so behind.

In order to keep himself out of sight till the last possible moment, Girton had knelt behind the desk, at the end nearer the safe and the door. Consequently, when he bobbed up he was able to grab the stumbling 'shield' and swing him aside.

As soon as the farmer's body swung out of line, Border brought up his weapons. Acting instinctively, Rudy grabbed his Winchester by the barrel and swung it against Border's head. Fortunately, it connected with the outlaw's temple before the six-shooters were firing. Border groaned, his eyelids flickered, and he slipped away to the carpet on the customer's side of the desk.

One glance was all Rudy had time for. Crouching and leaping he flung himself at the gaping door-opening, and just succeeded in getting through it unscathed as bullets bit into the framework of the gap and ruptured the hinges.

Schmidt was behind the counter, near the window still. He fired carefully as Girton flung himself to the ground and wriggled across the floor behind the doubtful protective barriers made by the prone tellers. Pilch, on one knee, at the main entrance, finished reloading and blasted off at intervals of a few seconds.

One teller squealed as a bullet from Deac nicked his shoulder. The cry spurred Rudy on. He reached the bench in the lounge area and flung himself behind it. Bullets continued to probe his position, but he had sufficient protection for a breather and to reload.

The room stank of gunsmoke by this time, and he found himself coughing. The farmer's wife coughed herself back to consciousness, and Pilch's aim was spoiled by a throat irritation.

Just as Rudy thumbed a shell into his last empty chamber, Link Border started to pump bullets from the back room, about a foot from the ground. He had no specific target and only sought to confuse the enemy.

Girton had to do a deft wriggle to get his butt out of the new line of fire. While he was busy, John Pilch sprang to his feet, flung himself through the double doors of the bank frontage, and cautiously went in search of the horses. Without them, the outlaws had no real chance of a getaway.

As Pilch danced down the stairs and ran, crouching warily, towards the alley where the horses were, Dick van Groot was still moving on the flat roof of the tailor's building. Dick was aiming for the front, so he could overlook the bank doors. One item which he had not considered imperilled his position.

The tailor's shop windows had coloured awnings. Pilch had crossed over sufficiently far to be screened by the sunshades before Dick had a chance to see him. Pilch was slow to release and take over the horses because he felt sure that Dick was in or near the alley and liable to shoot.

In the meantime, Girton continued to exchange lead with Border on the one hand and Schmidt on the other. Some of the bullets flew so close that his remaining unscathed was a near miracle.

* * *

Dick started to mutter to himself. "Girton, come on out of that bank if you still have breath left in your body."

He was on his knees, trying to see over the front of the awning at first-floor level and at the same time listening for any developments on other sides. His restlessness led to his undoing. He heard the horses on the move, also the hoarse exhortation coming from the lips of Pilch.

If the horses were on the move, that meant that the outlaws were preparing to rush out. So he rose to his feet, rifle at the ready, hoping to get in a shot at the horse-minder as soon as they came into view.

A sizable chunk of glass had fallen out of the bank window on the left side of the door. Sufficient for Link Border to see the silhouetted figure on the opposite roof through the gap. He called a warning to Schmidt, who was still located near the other window.

Four horses appeared. Pilch had cunningly placed himself in the midst of them to protect himself from any sharpshooting. Dick saw the horses. He hovered stiff-legged, waiting for a proper sighting on the man in the middle. His concentration was so good that he failed to react when Schmidt knocked out glass from his window and poked a rifle through it. His first shot caught Dick in the shoulder, and knocked him off balance.

Pilch glanced up, surprised, and half blinded by the sun. He was in time to see Dick van Groot do a slow-motion crumble and fall over the front edge of the building. His body was performing a somersault until it was brought up short by the stout striped awning over the men's shop windows.

Dick bounced, watched by Pilch and Border, and also by countless onlookers hiding away up and down the street. The body bounced again, but stayed where it was, trapped in a fold of the awning.

"Hurry it up, will you, Boss!" Pilch called. "It's now, or never!"

Border and Schmidt took it in turns

to keep Girton behind the bench by firing shots at it. Suddenly, the doors were wide open. Border appeared, framed in the opening: a tall, imposing restless twin-gunned figure, masked and watchful, his white vest flapping as his chest heaved.

"Come on, Deac!" he called over his shoulder.

Pilch mounted one horse, held another in close and raised a hand holding the reins of the other two. Schmidt fired a last shot in the direction of the bench and darted for the door. He had to put up his guns because he was carrying all three canvas money-satchels, and they were heavy.

One of the tellers called out hoarsely, "They're getting away!"

Girton cursed fluently, slowly rising to his knees. Outside, Schmidt heaved up two bags which were strung together. He swung them over the saddle of one of the spare horses. At the same time Link Border swung into leather.

Schmidt reached down to dirt level to grab the third bag.

A bullet ricochetted off a metal door-hinge and struck him in the back. Schmidt was bodily strong. As he started to sink to his knees, Border exhorted him to make another effort. Cursing hard, and flicking his mount with the reins, Border contrived to round the pack-horse.

Schmidt groaned with the effort of lifting the third bag. His strength was draining away, but he hoisted the bag to chest level and held it long enough for Border to grab it from him. In taking charge of the bag, however, the leader lost control of the spare horse, dropping its reins.

Due to Girton's inspired shot, off the door-hinge, and this piece of ill-fortune, the hurt gunman had lost out in a matter of seconds. The released horse pranced away, beyond the reach of those who could have used him.

A mixture of curses and farewells came from the lips of Border and

Pilch as they prepared to gallop away. Two left out of a party of six. They rode with their mouths open and teeth bared behind the cream bandannas which were scarcely of use any more.

16

UNKNOWN to any of the main protagonists fighting at the bank, the other surviving van Groot was only a few yards away. Many hours earlier Martha had sensed that this was a critical day, not only for Rudy and Dick, but also for herself and her personal yearnings in life.

Consequently, she had followed Girton into town and kept herself well away from the scene of the action until it was well under way.

During the later exchanges she had crept down the intersection between the tailor's establishment and Melindy's restaurant. She had on a grey shirt and a short riding-skirt, the colours of which enabled her to remain unnoticed until quite late on.

For a minute or two after Dick's body had fallen from the roof his fate had stupefied her. She had remained on her knees, her face in her hands, her head resting against an upright of the sidewalk awning near the restaurant.

It took quite a time for her to realize that his broken body had not hit the dirt of the street, but when it became clear, she found her courage returning, her wits sharpening.

The two escapers had scarcely covered five yards into the intersection with the baggage-horse between them when Martha came to life. She rested a revolver on a horizontal pole and fired off two shots at the gang leader. One of them tweaked his bandanna and the other severed a piece of leather belonging to the loot-carrying horse's reins.

Handicapped by the bag he had balanced on his saddle, Border sweated, shouted and cursed, pointing in Martha's direction. It was clear to her and to John Pilch that he had recognized her. As the three horses swept up the intersection, Pilch was the nearer of the two escapers to her.

Martha had mounted her grey gelding and had launched him clear of the sidewalk. Her next effort was to shoot while still moving, but that was a skill at which she had had no practice.

As Pilch's white mount swept by, he stiffened his right arm and levelled a six-shooter at her. He could not claim to be new to shooting from the saddle. The two guns were discharged at the same time. Martha's shot flew high and wide of the target, while Pilch's bullet homed in on the female rider.

The dappled grey shuddered, half leapt in the air and started to roll over, going down as it did so. Its involuntary action prevented another bullet from hitting Martha, who felt that she was hit. The trio of horses thundered on, and very soon only echoes, dust and gunsmoke remained . . .

★ ★ ★

Girton staggered out of the double doors just in time to see the demise of his sweetheart and her pony. Martha hit the ground rather heavily and stayed down, right alongside the dying grey's shuddering neck. The horse finally shuddered its last, and Rudy's heart felt as heavy as death.

He plunged across the intervening yards on leaden legs, ignoring the prone figure of Deacon Schmidt at the foot of the bank steps. All his thoughts were on the inert figure of his sweetheart. Nothing else existed until a bullet fired from the rear ripped away one of his boot heels, arresting his progress and making the adrenalin flow again. He turned, dropped on one knee and put a single bullet through the forehead of the dying Deacon, helping him swiftly into the next world.

Martha's eyes opened as he crouched over her, breathing like a defective pair of bellows. "Are you . . . ? Where did the bullet . . . ?"

Her face was pale, but her senses were rapidly returning. She managed to conjure up a smile, and shook her head. He wanted to believe that she meant she was not shot, but it seemed that he was asking far too much.

Eventually, he saw that the grey had absorbed the only bullet: that she was trapped by her skirt, and probably only bruised and dazed, otherwise. He had to heave against the dead weight of her beloved pony, and also gently pull on her leg. A portion of the short riding-skirt elected to stay under the corpse, but eventually the two of them stood up, ruffled, distressed, but intact.

"What of Dick?" she murmured.

Rudy shrugged. He supported her weight as they hobbled round the corner to find out. Above them, the awning suddenly ripped. Dick's rifle fell through it, and his body — only one arm functioning — slipped through it immediately afterwards. Between them, they caught him and lowered him to the boards.

Dick groaned. Blood from his shoulder wound had soaked his sleeve. Martha had stripped the wound bare and was applying strips of her incomplete skirt to it when the thunder of hooves came again punctuated by gun shots.

Rudy did not believe his ears. He ran to the intersection and saw for himself. "They're comin' back! That posse must have arrived after all!"

Martha went on trussing Dick's arm as if the situation was unchanged. Dick was pale, but composed. They had character, the younger generation van Groots, as well as other assets. As the desperate riders erupted back into their lives, Rudy dropped down into the dirt and put up his weapon.

His gun, aimed at Pilch, went off at exactly the same time as Pilch's own weapon. Rudy felt his arm jerk, as Pilch's bullet creased the skin of his upper arm. Pilch, for his part, leaned forward at an extraordinary angle and never recovered. Rudy's shot had entered his rib cage under the left arm. He plunged slowly to earth and stayed there.

The bank doors were closed again.

From right and left fairly large numbers of armed men, some mounted and some on foot, blocked off possible escape routes. Link Border acknowledged that he was cornered. He dismounted and turned his wrath in the direction of Girton and the van Groots. Rudy's shooting-arm was useless. He couldn't fire with his left. Dick's shoulder wound precluded any shooting from that side of his body.

Border, bare-faced now, laughed hysterically. "You two, the van Groots, brought about my change of fortune, but you'll die on the same day as I do! Today!"

Rudy sank down beside a post, feeling helpless. Martha hastily rolled away from her brother. She flipped up her skirt and whipped the Derringer from behind her garter. It was not a man-stopper, but the miniature bullet which she fired into Border's chest slowed him. Not to be outdone, brother Dick scooped up the heavier six-shooter dropped by Girton and hit the outlaw leader two times out of three, using his left hand.

When the echoes faded, the action was over.

* * *

In Melindy's restaurant, taken over as a clearing-station, the doctor tidied up the wounds and ordered drinks and food for the battered trio of survivors. He took coffee with them when his tasks were completed.

"You were lucky," the doctor remarked, unnecessarily. "Sam Callaway's horse went lame, so he didn't make it. The county sheriff and his men were delayed. The bank president fainted on the way to the local peace office, so *he* never made it. Will you, Girton, go back to peace keeping in town after all this?"

Rudy was hazy after coffee laced with liquor. He grinned sleepily at Martha, who spoke up for him. "He has a choice, nay, expectations, doctor.

He could become an executive in the business controlled by the family of his wife-to-be. Or, he could go to law school, if he was so inclined."

Girton put the fingers of his left hand through his hair. He looked nonplussed.

Dick said: "If he objected to the van Groots payin' his college fees, no doubt the thousands of dollars he will receive in payment for eliminatin' outlaws would more than pay his way."

After that, there was total agreement. A lawyer executive . . .

THE END

FIGHTING RAMROD
Charles N. Heckelmann

Most men would have cut their losses, but Frazer counted the bullets in his guns and said he'd soak the range in blood before he'd give up another inch of what was his.

LONE GUN
Eric Allen

Smoke Blackbird had been away too long. The Lequires had seized the Blackbird farm, forcing the Indians and settlers off, and no one seemed willing to fight! He had to fight alone.

THE THIRD RIDER
Barry Cord

Mel Rawlins wasn't going to let anything stand in his way. His father was murdered, his two brothers gone. Now Mel rode for vengeance.

ARIZONA DRIFTERS
W. C. Tuttle

When drifting Dutton and Lonnie Steelman decide to become partners they find that they have a common enemy in the formidable Thurston brothers.

TOMBSTONE
Matt Braun

Wells Fargo paid Luke Starbuck to outgun the silver-thieving stagecoach gang at Tombstone. Before long Luke can see the only thing bearing fruit in this eldorado will be the gallows tree.

HIGH BORDER RIDERS
Lee Floren

Buckshot McKee and Tortilla Joe cut the trail of a border tough who was running Mexican beef into Texas. They stopped the smuggler in his tracks.

BRETT RANDALL, GAMBLER
E. B. Mann

Larry Day had the choice of running away from the law or of assuming a dead man's place. No matter what he decided he was bound to end up dead.

THE GUNSHARP
William R. Cox

The Eggerleys weren't very smart. They trained their sights on Will Carney and Arizona's biggest blood bath began.

THE DEPUTY OF SAN RIANO
Lawrence A. Keating and
Al. P. Nelson

When a man fell dead from his horse, Ed Grant was spotted riding away from the scene. The deputy sheriff rode out after him and came up against everything from gunfire to dynamite.

FARGO: MASSACRE RIVER
John Benteen

The ambushers up ahead had now blocked the road. Fargo's convoy was a jumble, a perfect target for the insurgents' weapons!

SUNDANCE: DEATH IN THE LAVA
John Benteen

The Modoc's captured the wagon train and its cargo of gold. But now the halfbreed they called Sundance was going after it . . .

HARSH RECKONING
Phil Ketchum

Five years of keeping himself alive in a brutal prison had made Brand tough and careless about who he gunned down . . .